I0626543

Small Rain and Other Nightmares

Paula Johanson

Published by Doublejoy Books, 2020.

SMALL RAIN AND OTHER NIGHTMARES

First edition. June 30, 2020.

Copyright © 2020 Paula Johanson.

ISBN: 978-1777144234

Written by Paula Johanson.

Table of Contents

Small Rain 1

Blood Turn 5

Working in a Vacuum 9

If You Go Out in the Woods 19

Skyline 31

With a Screwdriver 43

Smoke and Bubbles Rising...75

Sleep 79

What Scares You? 83

Small Rain

My knapsack was starting to fade, the canvas wearing in places. It still shed most of the rain, and anyway I had the food and bottled water inside wrapped in plastic bags. Grocery bags, with the handles tied tight to keep out the wet – some survivalist camping gear. I'd be lucky to make it halfway.

It was still raining, a light mist that had kept up without stopping all week. My hood was gathered in tightly around my face, and the peak of my ball cap kept my eyes dry at least. Most of the time. Things looked a little blurry.

Hard to get a ride. No one came by. I picked up the pack and was about to walk down the shoulder when my gut started cramping again. There was a line of trees between the highway and a field. I started over to find some bushes to crouch behind.

Old habits die hard. And then, about the time I decided not to bother getting soaking wet in the wilting hedge, my gut decided the matter for me. Quickly I lowered my jeans and hunkered down beside the road shoulder. At least I was in time to keep this pair of jeans from getting soiled. Good. I didn't want to go to the trouble of getting more clothes. I shouldn't need anything but what I was wearing, until I got home.

The grass was wet, but a handful cleaned me. Gaah. I was turning into a real pig, but who cared what sort of godawful trail I left behind me? I got walking again, knapsack swaying, and my legs slowly lost that rubbery feeling. Walking did feel better than just lying around, waiting.

The road being quiet, too, that was good. Better out here than back where the sounds of rain and water echoed down Main and Davies.

Creepy to hear waves washing up on shore in False Creek, and my bike the only thing moving down Main. No pigeons, even. There weren't any birds out here, either, but that had to be the rain. They were off in their nests or wherever they go, maybe back in the weedy fields behind the hedges. Sure, it was hardly even spitting, but if it bugged me maybe it bugged them. Birds are like people that way.

It had been raining for a week. That bugged me all the time I was lying around inside, waiting. It didn't bug me much more to be walking in the rain, once I had set myself up to it and got a raincoat from my landlady's closet. Still, when I saw a gas station ahead, across the highway, I didn't hesitate about going indoors.

I looked both ways before crossing the tarmac. Dumbshit. Old habits again.

The pumps were wrecked – glass broken, one hose torn off. The lid where they take dip measures of the big underground tank was off, and there weren't any packs of cigarettes behind the broken windows. More of what lay behind me.

I looked in the door, careful of glass and motor oil from a crunched litre bottle. There was a coffee shop, not so smashed up. Some of the food would have gone bad, but chocolate bars or something would –

A woman stood behind the clean counter, wiping it with a white cloth. She looked up and saw me in the doorway. She folded up the cloth and put it away behind the counter, picked up her little notepad and pencil. "Can I get you anything?" Her voice was gravelly, but the Irish was still audible.

"Yeah, just something." I came in carefully. "Nothing special."

"Grill's out." She coughed. "I can get you a sandwich."

"Thanks." The sandwich was already made, wrapped in plastic. Kraft cheese slices. No mayonnaise, even. No, of course the fridge was out, too.

"Coffee?" The cup was cold. The coffee maker didn't have that little red light glowing on it, either. She must've used cold water, probably from the tap. If the water still ran out here.

"No, thanks. I've got some bottled water." I unpacked my second-to-last litre of Perrier and poured some into the dishwasher-scratched glass she set on a napkin beside my sandwich plate.

"That's a good idea, drinking that," she said, and the gravelly voice softened. "That's good for your health, it is."

"Yeah." My watch beeped.

"Have you got an appointment, now?" she asked, her broad face wrinkling up in amusement.

I shook my head, swallowed the bite I was chewing. "No, it's time to take my iodine pill."

She looked astonished. "You don't take goiter pills and all at your age?"

"It's for the fallout," I muttered. "The worst of it, anyway."

"That's the hard part, the hoping, isn't it?" She took her cloth out and wiped the cold coffeemaker. "Me, I couldn't be bothered to do something special like that. I'll just go on as I always have. Better than trying all that and having it not work anyways. ...Not that I'm saying you're wrong, mind. You go on doing what seems right for you," she advised me, one finger pointing before she turned to wipe a milkshake machine that was already gleaming. "Like, you're going somewhere. That's good. And I'm staying here, and that's right for me, too."

There wasn't much I could say. I finished the sandwich while she got a broom and began sweeping. After a minute she asked, "Have you heard any news on the radio, at all?"

"Uh, no." I put my water bottle away. "Have you?"

"Not a word. Anybody know more about what happened, maybe in Vancouver, eh?" She had swept the length of the counter and had a small pile of dusty glass shards at her feet.

"I didn't want to stop and talk with anybody I saw there," I admitted. "Aren't you taking a chance with me?"

She nodded and tsked, her tight curls bobbing about her broad face. "You got a lot better manners than the last ones. Bunch of wild lunatics, if you ask me."

"Maybe they're the guys who put my bike in their van and broke my glasses."

The glass shards rattled into her dustpan, and she straightened. "You can't go around with broken glasses," she said, deeply concerned. "Just hang on, there's some tape here. Maybe I can –"

"Nope," I said, as cheerfully as I could. "They're trashed."

"So you're going on, then? Going home? That's good. Where is home, for you?" she asked.

"My parents' place, up beyond Hope."

She looked at me, shivering as I stood up. "It won't be the same, you know. It never is, going home. They might not be –"

"I know. But I've got to check on them, and on –" I broke off, coughing. My throat was raw. She'd got me talking more than I had for days.

"Ah, you've got a sweetheart there, too, have you?"

I nodded, still coughing.

"Well, be sure to take that iodine pill your watch rang for and all. Do your best."

I swallowed the pill with the last drops from my water glass. She said, "You take care, now," as I headed for the door.

"You, too," I answered, and went out into the rain. The wind was blowing warm from the west, and the misty rain was still falling. Steam rose from the ground to meet it. I kept walking unsteadily, with my back to the wind.

Blood Turn

It's bothering me. The distinct odour of fresh blood on her breath is bothering me. I don't expect a small, plump, grandmotherly woman (but a well-kept grandmother) to smile proudly at her husband at the lectern and confide to me in a stage whisper that she's pleased by how we young people react to his lectures, while the cloying smell of blood clots rolls forth with her every breath. She makes me think of meat, and steak, blue-rare. Instead of the lecture or the conference, I think of menstrual blood in the shower, spiralling down the legs and around and down the drain. I remember hospital visits for my new babies' vaccinations, my brother's traffic accident and the blood donor clinic at this convention with first-timers, very white, leaving after their donations.

I know blood donors from both sides, friends at the clinic down the hall and remembering ... I know that rush of other-blood in my veins: a trickle where the flow should be loud, hard, and long. The pulse should hammer where it fluttered weakly and the drip drip drip was no substitute. There was a golden-skinned nurse at my side, measuring, soothing and cooling me with her hands, but the drip drip was somehow not antiseptic enough, for I could smell it. Or was it my own blood? I remember the hemorrhage and the dizzy darkness and the splash from crotch to ankles. Surely they had changed the bed after I had spiralled down into the dark. Then I smelled it; I smell it again now. This old woman brought it all back for me, the memory and smell of the fresh gush and clots of bright and dark and the musky, salty odour like the harbour at my door.

5

That's the tag that got this memory started, I realize. I live by the ocean, I smell it all day. Perhaps it's just that my neighbour in the next seat has a perfume or personal scent that's briny, and compelling like homesickness. She could even be wearing my mother's or grandmother's perfume. But then she leans forward confidingly again to whisper in my ear that her husband loves doing these talks, though it's such a bother to bring her along and so little for her to do at these conventions for young people and writers. I want to wipe my ear of the clot and trickle running from it. Her lips are unstained, even by lipstick – no need for it, her colour is high, even florid. Her hand grips a purse with no tremor, an easy strength in hands unknotted by arthritis.

She's like my grandmother: no arthritis. Strength in old age. I let the lecture run past me again and wonder how I can keep this friendly woman from unnerving me. Maybe I can get her to talk about herself and tell me stories like my grandmother does, my old mother, self/crone, my memory person who I am too much like already at the end of my youth. Last time I saw her was at Christmas, carving the turkey and setting out the bread and glasses of red wine at every place along the table. She held my babies and told me of her own mother putting binding bands on her children. She put no binding bands on my twins, but she wrapped me up tight. She told me stories while I wrapped twists of her white hair around my fingers into curls.

The smell of blood is becoming distressing.

The plump woman eases herself forward again to whisper of her husband's joy in these talks. She's glad it's something they can share, we all can share, even if she really isn't sure what all is going on. The sweat is starting out on me, and I don't know what all is going on. The milk pricks in my breasts and sweat gathers to trickle down my side, salt and sharp, but without that copper tang that is madness and release.

I knew release, remembered it from when my children were born – first one, then the other, release and an openness like I'd never known as the bewilderment and panic of my labour burst from me and flowed away. The man was on my right hand, the woman on my left hand; my children, male and female, turned small heads to follow their voices. And I was unable to hold them, open to the world as I went down into that twisting dark.

Turning, the plump woman strains to reach a dropped pamphlet. She is wondering aloud if young people really have respect for the aged anymore. I mutter something affirmative, thinking of my grandmother. When she said grace, our heads were bowed, but she looked upwards with eyes open. I wipe my hands with a tissue and remember what my grandmother told me to eat to keep the milk flowing sweet and freely for the babies, and how to wrap them warmly, for they came from a warm place. The blood scent is there still, and damn the convention, damn the talk and the people crowding the building, crowding the room and my space, I want to track that scent to its source. It's not my time, and that woman must surely be past it ... But she hands me the pamphlet and with her whisper again comes the hot smell of hunger, and distress, and comfort.

I can't face that need – not the distress and hunger and that need for comfort, for contact and binding around me and holding me. There is a moment of silence from the speaker at the lectern. In that quiet comes a rustling from the clothes and bodies of the people around me in the room, like that when my grandmother said grace, or when I told my family of the children I was carrying. When I look up, I see the change coming in this old woman's face as she lifts it to me like a priest lifting the Host. She is old, so old, but her eyes are young as a child's, and there is comfort in the set of her mouth. When she takes my hand, I feel the touch moving in me like the twins turning in me when I sang hymns in church at Harvest. With that I know who this stranger, this old woman, is for me; she is the Old Woman for me, Fate and Crone and Goddess for me, speaking in the flesh and the touch of hands. I know the comforting I must begin to give, and what she has just said that I did not hear. I twist out of the grasp of those strong, untrembling fingers and watch the white curls turn as I back out of the room, away from the crowded lecture and away from her words and unsettling breath.

At the end of the hall the young people move away from the phone for me. The coin drops, the dial turns under my hand and I will soon know if I can be there for my own old woman, my grandmother, when she needs me – like I needed her at the end of my youth.

Working in a Vacuum

It was another grey day. Under the lead grey clouds, a cold, light wind picked up particles of snow to brush against the storm windows. Only -25°C today on the thermometer. Around -20°F on the other scale. Warmed up some. The old furnace could make some progress toward fighting the cold. On cue, the furnace rattled and boomed and the fan came on, blasting hot air out of the vents. The walls were too cold to lean against, and the windows were still sandwiched in a layer of frost between the inner plastic film and the storm windows. Another winter's day. Maybe a little better than the last few, maybe not.

"OUTPUT IS DOWN FOR Number Six."

"Which one is that? What were we expecting?"

"There's a novel in progress, another outlined, and several short term projects and articles that should be completed soon."

"Oh, Number Six. Some of that will be what we want."

"But output is down."

"You sure? For how long?"

"The last few weeks. She sent only one 8x12 envelope from either of the post offices she customarily uses. That was a month ago."

"And how many #10 envelopes?"

"Two."

"Damn. She uses them for personal correspondence, too. Those were probably letters to her grandmother, not manuscripts."

"Don't knock it, boss. Some of those letters turn out to be first drafts for some pretty effective non-fiction."

"Pieces of fluff."

"With all respect, those pieces of fluff added up to three book-length manuscripts in two years. Two of which have already been sold."

"Your taste, not mine. The novel's the big project going right now. Check the progress on it and get back to me later."

THE TEAKETTLE WAS JUST coming to the boil. Tea with caffeine was the order of the day, to take the chill off and kick-start the mind into alertness. Maybe looking through the files of half-finished and recently completed writing would get something going. This mug had "Don't mess with me, bucko – I'm a WRITER" on the side. Sugar from the Bavarian china sugar bowl, with silvered handles cold from the cupboard and bright primroses on the bowl. Those were the only primroses that would be blooming around here for weeks to come.

"WHAT'S THE WORD ON the novel?"

"The three excerpts sent out as stories came back from two magazines and an anthology. And from the CBC Literary Contest."

"Everybody gets rejected by them. So what?"

"Yeah, boss, but the anthology rejection must have mattered more. I don't know if she did any work after that for some time."

"Not Six. Her standard response to a rejection letter is to prepare another manuscript and another copy of the rejected one and send them both out to someone else. Look at the files."

"Well, if that's standard, then there's something wrong. Nothing's been mailed out in over three weeks."

"Three weeks?"

"Almost four."

"She hasn't put *anything* in the mail in that long? And you're just getting around to telling me now?"

THE CUP WAS NO LONGER warming, but the caffeine was kicking in. Scrolling through files for half finished projects, nothing leapt out and demanded attention. Maybe it was time to read one of the books sent for review and send out the review on spec to some newspapers. Not much point in writing the review at this moment, though, not till the printer was up again. Better to work on some projects that wouldn't need to be printed out until later. Or hand-written notes about manuscripts sent out months ago that hadn't earned a response yet. Nothing old looked worth checking up on yet and nothing half done looked worth getting busy on. Damn, it was cold. Being cold even in two sweaters meant it was time for aerobics to get the blood moving.

"I CANNOT BELIEVE IT! Why wasn't this brought to my attention before now?"

"We've been awfully busy with Thirteen, boss. And you know what things are like for Eight and for Eleven right now."

"Excuses are useless!"

"I'd offer you excuses if I hadn't been busy doing my work. I've had my hands full, picking up all the pieces we want and checking on crises that needed action."

"May I remind you that collecting pieces we want is only part of our work? Careful, systematic monitoring may keep a crisis from developing that needs attention."

"So what do you want me to do about it now?"

"I want to get a look at the situation right away. Can we get a drive-by report?"

"Not really. Gas meter reader came by two weeks ago. Unless you want to send in Someone Seeking Directions or another Selling Frozen Packed Meat. We could arrange that in a day or two. "

"No, we did that back in November. Other unfamiliar vehicles on that stretch of back road will be unreasonably out of place. Whose idea was it to put a writer out in the sticks, anyway?"

"Yours."

"Mine?"

"You said it was a Canadian tradition."

"I must have had my head up my ass."

"You said something about urban pressures on the creative temperament."

"Don't remind me. Damn, we'll have to get a drive-by report from the utilities company truck. They go by often enough."

"There won't be one for a day or two. We'll have to get a drive-by from the grader."

"The grader ... Why from the road grader?"

"The road needs clearing. It was snowed in two days ago. Then the temperature dropped to -40."

"You didn't check in since?"

"Well, we've been tied up with Thirteen and that conference, and I thought..."

"To hell with waiting for a drive-by report from the grader. Get me the latest satellite photos."

"Right away."

"And utility consumption, gas, and telephone records from the last few days. I want to be absolutely sure she's still home and doing anything at all."

"You're worried, then."

"Damned straight I'm worried! In that climate, every winter somebody commits suicide by just sitting outside for an hour."

"Oh. I had no idea. Is ... is getting blocked *that* bad?"

"Find out if she's made any calls this morning."

AEROBICS GOT THE BLOOD moving, but it didn't do much else. Not very practical. Why was Sandy never around at times like this? It would be a really good idea to go back to bed, make love, and sleep. It looked like there wasn't a thing to do but something practical like shovelling out the driveway. Repetitive work like that was good for thinking out dialogue, anyway. By the time a chore like that was done the story practically wrote itself. That's if the hands didn't get too stiff. Time to bundle up even more. Snow pants. Felt-lined boots. Down vest. Coat. Toque. Two pairs of mitts. And where the hell was the manure shovel? The snow shovel wouldn't clear snowdrifts.

"UTILITY RECORDS SHOW higher than average consumption of gas and electricity the last three days."

"That's natural, it was -40. She probably stayed indoors, turned the thermostat up, and made pot after pot of tea."

"She made a phone call this morning and received another. Mechanic in the nearest town. And you wanted the latest satellite photos. This was taken on this morning's pass."

"Let me look. You didn't see anything to comment on here?"

"Everything looks quiet and normal."

"There isn't a new footprint in that yard or field and you think that looks normal? She hasn't stepped out of the house in three days!"

"Aw, come on, the porch has been swept clear."

"Clearing the porch is nothing! Five minutes, tops."

"So what?"

"So what? Don't you know Six *yet*? This writer's best pieces are written after long walks or dull, repetitive work. Particularly when alternated with meetings with other writers."

"Oh."

"Oh, yeah. And has she done any of that lately?"

"Uh, no. Not so far as we can tell."

"No long walks. No trips to the city to visit with other writers, to buy books and writing materials?"

"Uh... no. She hasn't used her Interac card in six weeks."

"Six weeks? You said it was four since she put anything in the mail."

"Almost four weeks."

"All right. What did she last use the card for, a deposit?"

"No, withdrawal. Bought bread, canned milk, and fruit."

"No writing supplies bought for several months either. Damn! She must be getting low on materials."

"Now, boss, don't worry about that yet. Remember how last year Six didn't buy any paper for months and you were worried she had run out and would get ... uh, stuck, when she had no paper?"

"Yeah."

"And it turned out when she helped a friend move house; the friend had given her a few reams of paper? Kept her going for months, remember?"

"Yeah."

"So maybe she is low on materials, but maybe not."

THE SNOW THAT FELL just before the cold snap was piled and drifted beside the porch stairs as high as the third step. First thing was to clear a path to the car. Funny how people depended on cars in this climate, away from the cities. There must be a story in that somewhere. Clearing around the car came next, and then the driveway. With the hands already stiffening, that would take hours. Maybe some today, some tomorrow. It's not like there was much getting written around here anyway. Working until the snow was all cleared was the thing to do. Might feel productive. But damn this cold. Warmed up to -25°C and still every breath stole heat out of the heart of you.

"NO NEW MATERIALS OR library books. No meetings with other writers in two months. Nothing sent out in the mail in a month."

"I admit it, boss, it looks bad now. I should have checked earlier. But we have been busy with that conference."

"That was only for the last couple of days. Now that we're aware of what's going on for Six, we have to get on top of it."

"So what will we do? This doesn't call for windfall money, does it? Or an unexpected sale to a new magazine starting up by a friend of a friend?"

"No, hold off on the windfall money. That's so impractical, it rarely has any reinforcing effect beyond the next meal or two. And we don't have time to set up a new magazine. We'd usually do that to benefit a couple of these writers at once."

"What's really happening for Number Six?"

"Right now? We can't be sure, unless we send someone in."

"I wonder what it's like for Six. I mean, writing. And living the way she does. I read her first book. And the stories."

"So did I. Try Thirteen and Four. You'll be surprised at the effect of different perspectives and circumstances."

"Why don't we just set up some kind of grant or bursary system instead? Something overt."

"Trust me. Running a store-front operation like that is a whole new ball of wax. Subtle is better. We hide out here, find out what we can, pick up what we want."

"Or we could commission what we like."

"Inspiration is an even more subtle thing. We'll go on getting what we like from among what gets published or broadcast. It's what we've always done. We find enough good stuff for all the travel, and the work, and the lonely times."

"But 90% of what they write is shit! Even these..."

"90% of everything is shit. You read Sturgeon?"

"Yeah, he was the one who for ten years was ... uh, blocked."

"Different department. Not my fault. I was an intern."

SOME OF THE SNOW WAS loose, some was crusted and the shovel took away more in each scoop. Hands and feet weren't cold anymore but they were still stiff. That meant they weren't warming up, they were freezing, even inside all this cold weather gear. Cold sweat was running down in three thin, pallid streaks under the gear. Clearing a few inches of loose snow with the snow shovel would have been nothing. Clearing crusted snowdrifts with the manure shovel got old real fast. Work like this was only a challenge and a chore for just so long. But after so much of it, clearing the driveway for the third time in a month was more than hard. It killed the joy in being outdoors, strong enough to do practical work. It killed the thoughts and words that ran on most of the time, and killed the writing voice with cold and stiffness. It felt futile to do this, when there would only be another storm next week to fill in the driveway again. And another. And sometimes holing up indoors at the keyboard felt futile, too, especially when the printer was down. Some days it felt like writing into a vacuum.

"I DON'T LIKE IT. SIX needs something today."

"Are you sure, boss? Maybe she's just re-reading Tolkien or quilting another blanket. It's winter, it's cold, and she doesn't have any contract to finish. It doesn't mean she's, uh, blocked."

"Six needs something. No long walks, no meetings ... She's not blocked. Not Six. She's out shovelling her driveway clear."

"At -25?"

"After being snowed in for three days? You bet your ass."

"Why would she shovel snow in that much cold?"

"To get the driveway clear, for Pete's sake. And to get her head clear, after three days indoors. To do the kind of repetitive work that gets her thinking before she writes."

"I simply do not understand the creative mind."

"You don't know anything about living on a planet, either. We're working in a vacuum here. That's why we get these stories from people who know. Now, we've got to do something about this."

"Well, it is a waste of time. She could be..."

"She could be killing her health. And people do die shovelling snow in that kind of cold."

"Oh, come on, she's a young writer. It's just a driveway."

"Young for a writer means only a few books. Get real. Six is not a young thing like you. That driveway is a hundred feet long."

"Oh. You think she'll have a heart attack?"

"Well, it won't do her heart and lungs any good. My own supervisor never forgave himself for Woodcock's health. A couple of cold winters meant pain for the rest of Woodcock's life."

"So what can we do?"

"That grader has a radio, for the dispatcher. Listen up."

THERE WAS A BIG, SLOW vehicle approaching, up the slope and along the half-mile behind the willows. Sounds carried far out here. It was the grader, come by at last after the cold snap. To see the big blade scraping a lane clear was encouraging. The grader would have miles to go today, to clear the roads in time for the school bus on Monday. Bet the driver was already stiff in his seat, with hours of work yet to do. Still, using a scraper blade like that beat all hell out of moving snow with a shovel. His hands wouldn't be this stiff.

As he went by, he waved. Then he backed and turned into the driveway, almost as far as the car, lowered the blade again, and scraped the driveway clear. In thirty seconds the grader cleared what would have taken hours with a shovel. Didn't the dispatchers tell the drivers to keep to a schedule, or didn't they charge a wad if they had time to clear a driveway? But the driver waved and headed out. And damn, if these cold hands were not too stiff to wave back after all. Who was that driver anyway? Looked like Ron Perlman, driving the Lone Grader. He sure wasn't working in a vacuum. And neither am I. Now why would he do that? That had to be the nicest thing to happen for weeks. Wonder what he was thinking, what he did at the corner where the big dog lives, what he'll do if ... I wonder if the milk's gone off yet or if it's still good enough to put in a cup of tea. I wonder.

If You Go Out in the Woods

When winter settled in around this country, it was strictly snowshoe weather for walking anywhere but on the trodden path to the stable or the kids' play area. For the walk into town, especially, whether I walked along the highway or cross-country, it took hours on snowshoes. The Slocan River was iced-up and the Valhalla Ranges were completely inaccessible. Maybe next year I'd get skis and learn how the Norwegians did it. Meanwhile, it was wool socks and boots and maybe I could still keep all my toes.

My son Kevin, who likes to do whatever I'm doing, was bundling up as well. We'd already debated whether or not he would accompany me to town and (thank God) had put that off till another time. Christmas presents and all. Maybe he could wait till the snow had gone – I wish. It's enough worrying about Kathleen here alone with little Alice without having to keep an eye on Kevin among strangers and roughnecks in town. But Kevin is sensible enough, for an eight-year-old, to know when it's better to stay home and safe. He even stopped insisting on Christmas lights when I promised him a red light bulb for the living room. All that, "Aw, please, Mom," when we have no front windows to hang the lights in.

"I'll follow you as far as the meadow," Kevin chattered. "Then me and Alice'll make a snow fort and tomorrow sneak out there and attack you when you come home." He helped Alice find the sleeves of her parka.

"Okay, sport." I found my mitts and wriggled my hands into them. "Scarf and toque, Kevin, it's cold out."

He gave me an exasperated look. "Aw, if me or Alice gets cold, we can just come home."

"*Smile* when you say that, pardner." I pulled the toque over his ears. "And it's 'Alice and I' as the subject of a sentence."

"*Smial*," he repeated. "Subject, object, predicate, clause; comma, colon, period, pause. Got it, Mom." Alice looked like a furry bear, all bundled up.

"We're ready to go." I looked for Kathleen, who came forward and hugged me, her body not yet awkward with the baby due this spring. "I'll be back tomorrow. You be careful, Kath – ask Kevin to get the schoolbooks from the top shelf this time, eh? No risking accidents." We left the kitchen, clumped through the mud room in our boots, and heard the door close firmly as Kathleen locked it behind us. "All right, kids," I commanded, "single file, forward *march*. 'I love to go a-wandering, along the mountain track...'" Kevin sang descant to my soprano and Alice tried to fa-la-la and val-de-ree where she could. The play meadow was a hundred yards from the house, its snow dimpled with old footprints only partially covered.

Both of the kids were picked up and thoroughly hugged. "Be good, honeybear. And you, sport, look after her. If you two go walking anywhere, play Good King Wenceslas, eh?"

"Sure, Mom," Kevin nodded. "But why should we walk in one set of tracks when no one's come by for years?"

"Because, Kevin," I put a hand on his toque, "the people who pass us by and go into town are hungry and don't have anywhere to live. If they know there are people here they'll come and hurt us and live here. Or maybe the Mackanness', or one of the other secret houses."

"Smiles," Alice corrected me. "Hobbit-hole, round in the ground."

"Yes, honeybear. So we leave very little for strangers to find. We don't want them to know we're here."

"What about Mr Harris at the store?" Kevin wanted to know.

"He knew about us before. And his sister is Mrs Mackanness, so we trust him, and he trusts us not to make an avalanche fall on his store." I patted both kids again. "Now I'm going. Goodbye till tomorrow." They called goodbye after me, Kevin's clear voice and Alice's slurring cry. She had learned to talk a lot better in the past year, but she was still only Six. Maybe with time, and if she had enough protein to make her brain grow ...

Ah well, there were soybean seeds on my shopping list and the fish biocosm was at last working efficiently. We could eat a fish every week this winter and still not deplete our breeding stock. And Bossie would be giving milk again when she had had her calf. So it would be powdered milk til spring. At least we didn't have to keep the kids indoors all the time anymore, so they could get some vitamin D from the sun.

I soon left behind the smooth mound of our house, with its snow-covered saplings growing in the soil insulating the concrete shell of our roof. Settling into a steady stride, I set a good pace on the snowshoes. In the past, the strain of the awkward motions had sometimes sent me into writhing belly cramps but my period wasn't due for at least a week, so this time I had no trouble. I passed the Mackanness' smial around noon. We all called our half dozen underground homes in the hills *smials*, after Tolkien's hobbit books. It was a safety measure: if someone heard the kids chatter in town about "going home" (or if, God forbid, they were caught by someone in the woods) the words "going to smile" would only confuse the uninformed. The town was only five miles away, after all, though that short distance took me several hours to cover in the deep powder. It was late afternoon before I cached my snowshoes behind Harris' store and went in to do the Christmas shopping.

Harris recognized me at once, even under the ski mask that Kathleen had knitted me this fall. He stocked up the wood stove for the customers who were warming up nearby, then came and helped me with the list my family had made. It had been condensed but even so it was still a long list. We spent some time gathering cloth, needles, precious salt. Business was slow today; Harris ignored the browsers and chatted with me.

"Honey candy for the little ones?" he asked. "And what about some pickled cukes for Kathleen?" Harris had been quite solicitous of Kath since she had come to town and conceived his son's child. Now that young Peter was gone on the road to Vancouver, all Harris would let himself hope was that there would be a grandson he could call Pete.

"Those home-pickled cukes would be good. And a very little of the honey candy," I told him. "I want Kevin and Alice to keep their teeth. Maybe you have some apricots left from Vernon? We wrap them in paper with pictures drawn on it and tuck them in the stockings."

Harris chuckled. "Like the old mandarins we used to get."

"Well, it's a change from our apples. Speaking of which, here are the dried apple rings and fruit leather you wanted this time. And the wolf wool sweater that Kath knit. I hope your wife likes it." My pack now empty, I began to load it with the cloth, food, and other items.

Harris stroked the sweater admiringly. "Fine job she did. It was lucky to get the fur – that the beast didn't kill you both instead, Janice." I looked up at my name. "I told you to carry a gun when you're up there. How a knife ever did the job, I'll never know."

I grinned, sliding six inches of steel out of my sleeve into an easy grip. "Oh, hell, it's not as if it was a true wolf. It looked as though a Samoyed ran wild and had half-breed pups. While it had its jaws clamped on my arm I knew it couldn't kill me right away, so I held its head till Kathleen came and cut its throat. Knowing it couldn't kill me till it got loose made it easier." I put the knife away without the other customers noticing it. "Kevin made a drum out of the skin. All by himself: he shaped the wood and tightened the skin. And, he made little fur cuffs for Alice out of the scraps. He's doing well."

"And is Alice any better?" Harris was studiously wrapping the honey candy that he knew she loved. I looked around; there were only one or two strangers in the store and they were out of earshot.

"She's talking pretty well now, but Kath is sure she'll never get much better than a four-year-old. Like I told you, we figure it's an enzyme she's missing, some PKU thing. A real hospital could have fixed it at birth. The food she ate as a baby never built her brain up properly; wouldn't have even if we'd let her drink Bossie's milk when she was weaned, in spite of fallout." I accepted the candy and tucked it in the pack. "But there'll be milk again with the new calf. I should tell Jack Miller that his bull did the trick, and next year we'll breed a calf for him. I do wish Kathleen had settled on a better stud fee."

"How about the stud fee you owe my son Pete?" Harris poked me. "Don't that beat all, Kathleen coming in with Kevin and Bossie and heading home with both them girls knocked up. I bet Kevin had some questions after that, eh?" He burst into laughter. "And when'll it be your turn, Janice?" He poked me again with an arthritic finger.

The old devil. It was funny enough, but I laughed less than he did. "Not till Kath's baby is three or four years old. Maybe I'll have a new husband by then," I said somewhat soberly. "I still miss Steve. I know Kath misses Mike, too, though Peter went a long way to helping her get over that. Now he's off to Vancouver and the ships, God bless him. Who knows what Vancouver's like since the fallout? I hope he gets past the highway raiders."

One of the strangers had come nearer and Harris put his gnarled finger to his lips. "Talk softer, Janice," he warned. "These are travellers if not raiders. You never know for sure." The fellow went back to the wood stove and Harris went on. "They came in asking for gasoline around noon, insisting even after we told them we save it for emergencies. Well, rather than have ourselves an emergency on the spot, we sold them a few litres at the highest price we dared ask. And they paid it so easily I don't know whether I should have asked for more or turned it down as loot. You ask my wife tonight when you stay with us and she'll show you a ring for every litre."

I shivered. "Wolves are one thing, but men turned thieves and raiders give me nightmares." When Kath had dressed my arm from the wolf's bite and rocked me to sleep that night, my dreams were not of wolves but of men with teeth tearing at my arm and claws at my belly. "Um, oh, I nearly forgot. Have you got a red light bulb? I promised Kevin we'd put one in the living room."

Harris nodded and started to answer when a voice came from behind me. "Yeah, a red light for the whore's window." It was one of the young travellers. "Ask *me* for a kid, babe, I don't charge stud fees." He showed yellow teeth in a sparse beard. Harris should have known better – a raider can be known on sight. Young men travelling, sometimes on foot but usually in a decrepit hand-repaired Land Rover or van; skin and bones from irregular diet, eyes glazed or dilated from whatever drugs can still be found. And the clothes – you'd never see Peter Harris in blue jeans and a silk shirt (both filthy). Not all young wanderers were raiders but ones this dirty, skinny, and strung-out were the likeliest.

Shock at his attitude stopped me cold for a moment. No man had talked to me that way for six years. There were no police since a few strategically placed nukes had taken out enough cities that there wasn't any government left to speak of, but the locals didn't put up with anyone bothering women. When I started to move, Harris put a hand on my arm (right over the knife-sheath, the cunning devil). "That's family you're talking about," he snapped. "Dry up and leave. I don't need any more of your business."

I turned my back on the parting fellow and said clearly, "Well, I'll be off on my other errands now. I'll see you later this evening?"

Harris nodded. "Go right to my house when you're ready," he said softly. "I'll bring your pack and snowshoes when I close up." I walked out past the young raider.

The errands took as long as I could linger over them, trying to cool down. Imagine calling the mother of a home a whore. Imagine threatening her with sex she didn't want. He was lucky to be breathing after that. Last year even the gentle potter had joined the fight when some stoned stranger had raped Jack Miller's daughter. The anger passed. I walked to the Harris'.

Once inside the house I found the old couple both scared blind for me. "He must have overheard us talking," Harris explained. "My wife heard him and the other talking in the repair shop."

His wife, small and withering, nodded. "I heard them say they're going to wait on the highway till they see you leave tomorrow and follow you home. They know you've got family and things up in the hills."

"They're not going to steal from the town, break into one of the empty houses?" I asked.

Harris shook his head, knotted hands shaking as his wife brought in mint tea. "Too many people, too organized. They don't want to face the lot of us. They heard about electric generators and they want one for their Land Rover. They figure a place out of town like yours or my sister's will have one."

"That's stupid. They have to power the generator somehow. Most of us use small streams. Besides, first they have to find a smial," I used the hobbit-word we all knew. "And then they'd have to adapt the generator, and I bet they don't know how." After a moment's thought, I added, "They probably won't even be able to find a smial in all that snow."

"Whether they can or can't, they'll try. They could destroy your home and family." Mrs Harris poured steaming cups of mint tea. "Janice, I wish you all had come to spend this winter with us. If Kathleen is going to stay here from February till the baby comes in May, I don't see – "

"We couldn't leave the orchard that long." I tried to soften the dry tone of my voice. Why could I never remember her first name? "It's not just a house, you know that, it's a cycle that has to be maintained at all stages. If the wrong algae gets into the fish ponds, the fish die. If we turn off the generator, the hydroponic garden dies. Our stream may run dry or freeze over. If we even just let the house grow cold, it'll take weeks to bring it up to a comfortable temperature – and we don't even have a skylight like the Mackanness'."

Shifting in his seat, Harris had little more to say. "You may live in a hole in the ground," he muttered finally, "but you're part of our lives here. If you need help, we'll get some men and do what we did for the Millers when they were threatened – "

"Not yet," I snapped. "They don't know where any of the smials are, so they're no real threat. Do you want to kill them for standing on the highway?" The mint tea wasn't any help. I wanted coffee. There wasn't any coffee. "If we kill them out of hand, we aren't even defending ourselves." I kept seeing the wolf/Samoyed, watching us, stalking for minutes before it leapt. "We'd be just like them. I don't work that way. And what would that tell the kids about the way people should react to threats? Great object lesson. I'd rather avoid the issue entirely." The old couple waited for my magic solution. I thought about it. "If I leave now, they might not be on the road yet. At any rate, I'll stay off the highway. Full moon'll light the path, and the breeze I noticed coming in might even fill in my tracks before daybreak. They won't know where I've gone and, if your sister's skylight has stopped leaking heat, there won't even be a ripple of warm air to give away the smials."

They didn't like it, but I left.

The breeze had indeed come up a bit and was already filling in my tracks from the afternoon. By the time the raiders thought to check the woods, there'd be no sign of my passage.

Over the first hill I saw a glow, not silver like the cold moon rising but red and green and gold – goddamn Christmas lights, for Pete's sake. The Mackanness' kids must have pestered their mother into putting up the goddamn lights, just like Kevin had pestered me. They were older and remembered more. Well, it *was* pretty. And the glow from town would mask it if the light shone above the hill.

Which goes to show how a mind relaxing will slip into old rhythms. The town below no longer had lights after dusk, and without them the coloured glow would be clearly visible from the road. I trudged along, watching the pretty glow, and well after midnight came upon my own smial.

The vaguely circular hill pleased me aesthetically. Like a fool I tromped boldly around it, admiring how well our home suited the forest life. This was the way people were made to live: within the environment, not in spite of it. This and other profound statements occupied my cold-befuddled mind until I finally got around to knocking on the door, being in no state to try the alternative entrance by the stream.

It was Kathleen who pulled me in, unbundled me, and checked my feet and face for frostbite. She warmed me slowly, in a week's ration of warm water, and cursed me black and blue for coming home this way, raving at her about the pretty lights. I slept through most of it, but she had more in the morning, variations on the theme of "travelling on an empty stomach," "changing plans," and "what the hell were you thinking?" She'd already fed Bossie and the kids by the time I got up to explain.

The idea of the raiders waiting for me shut her up right away, and terrified the kids. When Alice clutched Kath's shirt and started to howl, Kevin grabbed and hugged her, wide eyes meeting mine over her head. "What were the pretty lights, Mom?" he asked. "I heard you telling Momma Kath about the pretty lights on the way home, while you were in the tub warming up." I could see the change in my face in the way he held Alice tighter. Dear God, the Mackanness' lights ...

This time Kevin came along and I didn't argue. He could hide as well as any deer by now, and he'd tell Kathleen if anything happened to me. It was noon when we reached the Mackanness' smial, and from first sight I could tell there was something wrong. Heat waves rose steadily from the skylight, where the coloured lights still glowed dimly. Kevin hid while I crept up and peered through the broken plexiglass. The room within held clutter: a broken punch glass, a scrap of silk. No doors had been forced, and no one was in sight. Asleep in the other rooms, no doubt. The Land Rover was parked next to the air intake, by the stream that powered their generator. I went back and got Kevin to help me.

"Watch carefully and say nothing," I warned him. We took a tarp from the Land Rover and covered the skylight, packing the edges with snow. Another tarp we rolled into a tube from the exhaust pipe to the smial's air intake vent, and sealed with silicon gel from the raiders' own repair kit. Then we gouged out a rough new path for the stream, pulled the pins on the Rover's hood and used it to dam the flow, redirecting it away from the generator. Inside the smial, as the generator died, the power-controlled doors slammed shut, probably waking the raiders and whoever they'd left alive this long.

"Now, Kevin," I said, turning to my son, "this is how an engine is started." The keys were gone, but I showed him how to hot wire a car, just as Steve had shown me before Kevin was born. We were in no hurry; the security system locked all internal and external doors in a power failure. Each room vented to the air intake and had a hidden exit. Any surviving family members would either escape or smile to watch their captors die. I started the engine and let it run. We waited.

Ten minutes later, a small head poked through the snow: the Mackanness' little girl emerging from one of the secret exits. Wrapped in a sheet, with a black eye and one ponytail missing, she looked around, saw us, and came over, barefoot in the snow. "They're in Momma's room," she whispered as we wrapped her in some of our clothes. "Nobody else is left. Will Momma die asleep?"

We told her yes. She nodded, curled between us. I thought about my apple trees. Last January I had burned smudges at night to make fog so the frost wouldn't kill the orchard. Sheila Mackanness came over in the dark of night to tell me the smoke was visible against the sky. I thought about my apple trees.

"Now you can come home with us," Kevin told the girl, rubbing her feet like Kathleen had rubbed mine.

"Smile when you say that, pardner," I chided him, watching the lights that no longer shone green and gold ... and red.

Skyline

One of the roosters crowed at almost the same moment that the alarm went off. I stuck one arm out of the covers and batted at the clock until the alarm shut off. On the other side of the bed, my husband's clock radio clicked on, blaring the 5 a.m. news and weather report.

Our morning routines were very different. He listened to the weather forecast before getting up to let the chickens out and check the beehives. I lay there, groggy, listening to the CBC morning show for another twenty minutes after he left.

When I finally got up, I still had time to boot up the computer and boil water for tea and porridge before getting dressed. Duncan came back in to find me drinking Earl Grey and typing headlines into a file I keep for story ideas.

"There was another mole in the trap this morning." He left his boots behind the door. "Jo, did you catch the news earlier? That cop was convicted of sexual assault. And they're dragging the North Saskatchewan for someone who fell off the High Level Bridge."

"Foul play?" I entered both headlines into the file.

"They don't think so. Any hot water left?" He picked up the kettle and swirled it to see if there was enough water for a cup of coffee. "Uh, Jo, what are we planting today?"

I put down the cup of tea - it was still too hot anyway. "Let me save this file and I'll boot up the disc with the plans we made."

"Why don't you ... oh yeah, we've only got the one computer working." When the water poured into his cup, I could tell he was using

31

one of those flavoured instants. The smell was tempting, but coffee never tastes as good as it smells. "Damn, I don't want to have to go to town this week."

There was a sound from the kids' room; one of them was turning over. Nothing I had to get up for. "We wouldn't have to drive that far if they sent the disc drive out by mail." I began retrieving the file he wanted.

"*Ha ha chuckle ha.* Wait two more weeks for a delicate piece of hardware to arrive broken?" The cupboard closed; I looked round the doorjamb to see him adding rolled oats and Sunny Boy to the pot of hot water, making porridge.

I turned back to my keyboard. "Too bad we can't just order it and pick it up from the mailbox, like that spring that came yesterday."

"Wrong size." Duncan stirred the porridge grimly, wooden spoon in one hand, coffee mug in the other. "I tried it and it doesn't fit the rotary tiller. Gear shift keeps going into neutral or reverse." He went to the kitchen window over the sink. "Jo, will you come stir this? Someone's pulling into the driveway."

I turned off the heat under the porridge while Duncan got back into the rubber boots he wore around the yard. "Who'd come visiting before six in the morning?"

"Well," Duncan grinned for a moment, "my folks are at the farm conference in Brussels, so it's gotta be strangers." He went out to see who it was and what they wanted. It was time to wake and dress the kids, so I was busy for the next several minutes. The twins, t-shirts askew over shorts, were saying grace over their porridge when Duncan came back in.

"Feel like rustling up a big breakfast?" he asked, his grin back and bigger than ever. "It's a car full of people who want to stock up, buy a picnic lunch and a farm breakfast. There's six of them out at the picnic table by the playhouse."

"The dog and her puppies sleep under the playhouse," Bobby commented around a mouthful of porridge.

Josie nodded and swallowed. "She let us pet the puppies again yesterday," she informed me.

I leaned around two six-year-old heads and grinned back at Duncan. "If the dog doesn't mind, why should I? But maybe they should come inside to eat."

"They want to eat outside. There's no mosquitoes out, at any rate." His baseball cap slipped forward and he pushed it back. "I'll tell them you're working on breakfast, all right? You kids help your mom, I'll be busy fixing the rotary tiller."

I had the fridge open and was already pulling out eggs and green peppers. "I'll keep your breakfast warm," I said, but the screen door banged and he was outside. "Are you kids done yet? Josie, can you take a box of apple juice out to the picnic table? Bobby, please take six glasses out, too — that's right, the new plastic ones. Thanks, kids."

Making breakfast was a production. I tried to tell myself, when I had hash browns and scrambled eggs and a new pot of porridge cooking all at once, that it was good experience for if we ever opened a bed-and-breakfast like we'd been considering. When the toaster popped I was sending the twins out with a tablecloth, plates, bowls and cutlery, but somehow I got around to everything and even brought out all the food while it was still hot.

They were nice people — didn't seem to mind the kids setting the table or that their "waitress" was wearing jeans and a man's workshirt. One of the men was straightening his knife and spoon when I brought out the scrambled eggs. "That smells great," he said. The sleeves of his white shirt were already rolled up to the elbow. "We're so glad you were willing to put on a spread like this for us."

The others nodded agreement, passing platters around the table. Soon each of them had a bowl of porridge as well as a full plate. I made a mental note to make more toast, and open another jar of saskatoon jam. "The coffee'll be ready in a minute. Oh, and my name's Jo, and these are — "

"Josie and Bobby. They already told us," one of the women said with a smile. "They also showed us the puppies — after they set the table," she added quickly. "Uh, I'm Janice, and this is Carol, Tim, Michael, Kim, and the greedy guy there is George."

"Thanks a bunch," said George, putting the platter of hash browns down.

The twins ran past, chasing a rooster. "Are you just out for a picnic today or travelling somewhere?" I asked, with one eye on the twins and the other looking for the empty juice container.

"Oh yeah," said Michael, the one who seemed to like my scrambled eggs. "We wanted to get way out somewhere that would feel like the middle of nowhere to us." None of them were really dressed for the outdoors, but at least the women were wearing slacks and flat shoes.

"It sometimes feels like the middle of nowhere to us, too." I was thinking that the next time I would wear anything but jeans and workshirts would be in two or three weeks, when we drove to town to pick up the new hard drive. "When I give people directions, I usually just tell them we're one mile west and one mile north of the Wildlife Park."

"No kidding?" Carol, or Kim, stopped spreading honey on her toast. "Lions and tigers and bears ..."

"And wolves and a giraffe. We can hear the big cats roaring on a quiet night. It's less than a mile away, cross-country." I looked around the table and saw that they all had enough of everything, except toast and coffee. "The coffee's ready by now. I'll bring it out."

After that I spent some time putting together a picnic lunch for them. Through one window or another I could hear the kids moving around: one climbing a tree, the other running with a kite. One of the visitors, Tim maybe, left the picnic table and helped get the kite up into the air. George and Carol were over looking at the rotary tiller with Duncan when I brought him out his blue spackleware mug full of coffee.

"Your porridge is still warm," I told Duncan. His hands left smudges of black grease on the mug. "Any chance you'll come in and eat it soon?"

The tiller was tipped forward and the stench of gasoline couldn't be completely covered by the coffee. "This is no problem, except for the spring." Duncan passed me back his mug. I took it gingerly, avoiding the smudges. "I'm trying to see if I can cut it down to the size of the old spring." He held the spring, with its broken hook, beside the new spring for comparison.

"Is that the size you want?" asked Carol. "Because I think there's one rolling around in the glove compartment. Let me get it and see if it fits." She walked quickly in her leather city shoes across the yard to where their Nissan Multi was parked next to our lilac bushes. After rummaging in the glove compartment for a minute she pulled out a paper bag, tore it open, and shook out a heavy spring.

It turned out to be the right size and was even painted the same red as the tiller. "Looks like I get my breakfast after all," Duncan wiped his hands on a rag and passed it to me so I could wipe his smeared mug. "I'll be able to till between those rows of peas this morning, now that the spring works. What can I give you for it?" he asked Carol.

She shook her head. "It's nothing, just something we had rattling around. I wouldn't hear of payment after that great breakfast."

"You should really go and get yours," George suggested. "Don't let us keep you from it."

Duncan went in to have porridge and more coffee, and I went over to clear the picnic table. Janice, Kim and ... um, Michael all had their heads bent over a map spread out between stacks of plates and bowls. Kim looked up as I loaded a tray with empty platters and juice glasses.

"That was terrific. I never had green peppers in scrambled eggs before. And you sure had all the food ready fast. Do you do this often?"

"Just for family, so far." I stacked plates and bowls and made a heap of cutlery on one end of the tray. "We're hoping to open a bed-and-breakfast, maybe this winter. You know, farm vacations for people who've never lived on a farm in their lives?" Kim nodded; Michael and Janice were still lost in the map they were studying. "It would be some income to supplement the market gardening and writing."

"You're a writer, then? What do you work on, an IBM?" Kim put coffee mugs on the tray and helped me balance it. I managed to lift the tray without wobbling too much.

"Actually, we have two identical computers. Mine's for writing and personal files — I'm working on a program to generate story ideas out of current event headlines. We got Duncan another machine for farm records and his own files, but the disc drive needs to be replaced so we're down to one system again for a while." I would have to get the tray back inside sooner or later. Time to see how well I had piled the dishes. They teetered a bit, but didn't fall.

"Oh, Jo?" Janice was folding up the map so a route marked in pen was on the outside. "Do you have an outhouse or something?"

"You can come on inside to the bathroom," I suggested, the tray growing heavier every second.

"Oh, no, I don't want to intrude. Is that an outhouse or whatever?" She pointed and I nodded.

"You're welcome to it, if you want. I've got to get this inside." Somehow I got across the lawn, up the porch stairs, and into the house without dropping anything. The tray clunked onto the kitchen table and I decided to leave it until after our visitors had left with their picnic lunch. The sandwiches, juice, fruit salad, and potato salad all packed pretty neatly into a carton we had gotten with our latest grocery order. I must have become an expert while packing picnic hampers for the four of us. This bed and breakfast idea might work out pretty well after all, I decided.

Even with paper plates and disposable cutlery the carton wasn't too heavy or awkward to lift. I carried it onto the porch and looked around to see if anyone was ready for it yet. Janice was rummaging in the back of the Multi and she waved me over to her.

"Have you got room for this in back?" I rested one corner of the carton on the bumper. She moved boxes around, lifted a small one out, and made room for the carton. "There — that'll be easy to get out later when you want to stop for your picnic. Any idea where you'll have lunch?"

"Oh, not too close by." She smiled and nudged me. "You'll never guess what I've got here."

"Probably not," Bobby was swinging by his knees from a tree limb and yelling like a maniac. If I went over and told him to be careful, he'd insist he was. Sometimes it was better not to look. "What is it?"

"A disc drive. Want to bet it'll fit in your computer?" Her grin was as bright as Josie's. "Try it out."

"What?"

Janice pushed the box into my hands. "C'mon. My brother upgraded his home computer and gave me a few pieces to trade in or recycle or whatever. It's hardly been used, and it didn't cost me a cent. See if it will work."

I shrugged and took it in to try. Duncan stood aside and held the door to let me in, then clomped out in his rubber boots. Before long I was back out, looking for him.

He and Michael and Tim had their heads under the hood of the Multi. "That's got it," said Duncan. "Shouldn't give you any more trouble now." He closed up his tool kit as Tim closed the hood.

"Duncan," I said quietly at his elbow. "Janice just gave me a disc drive for your computer."

"Oh yeah, Michael was saying something about she had a free one from somebody. Will it work?" He had been wanting his machine back on-line for days.

"It ought to," I told him. "It's the right one."

His eyes widened. "The same as the old one? Numbers and everything?" At my nod, he laughed. "What a fluke, eh? I wonder what the odds are of that."

There was something else I wanted to talk about, while the visitors were busy piling into their vehicle. "How much did they pay, for lunch and breakfast and all?" He showed me a small wad of twenties. "Duncan, that's too much ... especially with the disc drive. We should—"

"We should accept it," he finished for me. "George says it would have cost them more than this to buy the meals in town and waiting for a mechanic at the nearest gas station would have been boring and expensive. He told me it was worth it and, besides, he didn't want a stack of charge card receipts to handle. I even sold him some gasoline. It's all under the table and off the record. Look, they're saying good-bye to the kids. Put your happy face on and say good-bye."

We smiled and waved, and they all waved back, but they didn't look as if they were off on a holiday. Except for Janice, who winked as she rolled up the front passenger window and spread out her map, they all looked more grim and determined than cheerful. The kids waved and shouted as the Multi rumbled off our driveway and down the gravel road.

"Wow, Mom. This was almost like Uncle Karl's visit on his way back east." Josie's short hair swung as she shook her head in amazement. "Real quick and busy."

Well, it was quick and it was busy, but now that they were gone the dishes had to be done. Duncan was already starting the rotary tiller, so I went inside and began washing the dishes. Later, about half-way through one of the frying pans, I heard the kids calling out, "A deer!" in delight. I looked out the window. It wasn't a deer, not with those spiralling horns.

I shouted for Duncan just as he shut off the tiller. "Jo! Get the kids inside!" He pulled off his earmuffs and I saw the headphones of his music player. "Kids! Go to your mom!"

Dripping soapsuds, I opened the screen door for the kids. "Did you see the gazelle?"

"It's not just gazelle. I've been listening to CBC radio. They interrupted the morning show with a special announcement. There's been trouble at the Wildlife Park and some of the animals have escaped." He left the tiller where it had stopped and came up on the porch. "All the big cats."

He came in and latched the door with the catch that was out of the twins' reach. I turned on the radio, for once not listening to the warm voice of the radio host. All I could think of was the tiger, lions, and bear pacing in their cages, looking out through the bars with hatred. A helicopter drummed its way nearer, overhead.

The kids were excited and so tired of being indoors that by evening they had wound themselves up tighter than the spring in my alarm clock, before finally falling bonelessly asleep. That morning and afternoon we had heard helicopters again several times, and trucks in Armed Forces green rumbling down the gravel road. By evening the casualty reports were coming in and repeating every half hour.

The giraffe at the petting zoo broke his neck during a chase. A police officer was trampled by a wood buffalo but survived. All the big cats that had gotten out were captured within an hour by Armed Forces and a special weapons teams — but not before tragedy struck, as the CBC reported the mauling of six people who were picnicking near the Wildlife Park.

"It was a good thing I had the headphones on when that report came through," Duncan said. "The twins didn't need to hear it ... oh God, all six of them ..."

"We had to turn off the radio anyway or the kids wouldn't eat." I shivered. "We can't even play the regular news during dinner. It scares the kids too much. Husbands shooting wives, cops assaulting suspects ... even a lost kid sounds scary to the twins. The news reports scare me, too, honestly."

"Yeah, but that's how we heard about the animal escape and knew to get inside." Duncan was quiet for a while. "It's hard to think of it — all six of them killed by one angry tiger. How many dead is it now? We've heard about so many people killed this year." The heat was going out of the day, and we had both doors propped open to the breeze. There were only a few gazelles still at large. "Did you hear? The First Nations people who run the Wildlife Park say this was an organized release by people who wanted to look like animal rights activists."

"Weren't they?" It was getting darker. I could see the level line of the horizon against the dim sky.

"The activists had the right t-shirts and slogans, all right, but they're reported to have carried the same weapons as the special tactics personnel."

"Activists use bolt-cutters, not — " I pulled my hair in frustration. "What sort of imagination have I got? I couldn't make that up if I tried."

"That's why you have the headlines program: to generate story ideas, get you thinking." Duncan's reflection in the kitchen window showed him coming up behind me. He rubbed my shoulders for a minute. "Maybe you should enter the latest headlines into your file."

I turned to do that, and he patted my neck. "I don't know what sense any program can make out of all the news I cram into it. Food bank statistics. Welfare cuts. Immigration scams. Cabinet shuffles." I went and booted the program, working on automatic pilot while my voice ran on. "And aspartame makes 2% of the people who ingest it have headaches and lower IQs. Dunno what all's going on with the world."

The floor creaked as Duncan went from window to window, looking out. "Almost enough to make you believe in government conspiracies, eh? Why don't you sort your data for conspiracies?"

"In a minute. I'm entering headlines about the Wildlife Park and — our guests." I closed my eyes for a moment, then grimly bent over the keyboard again. "All right," I said a little later. "What shall I sort for? State conspiracies?"

"Too broad. What about senseless deaths correlated with government conspiracies? There's a lot of murder reported in that file of yours." Duncan leaned over the back of my chair. "Maybe some of the facts will correlate."

"I'll get it to print out the relevant headlines in chronological order, most recent first."

While I was busy, Duncan muttered, "Inverse chronological order." I swatted at him and told him to quit reading over my shoulder. It didn't take nearly as long as I thought it would before the printer was busy.

The first item read, "Tragedy strikes Wildlife Park. Six mauled by tiger during release of animals by persons unknown." The second item was about infant mortality rates on Canadian Indian reserves. I couldn't read any further.

Maybe we were both feeling a little sick. Duncan and I ended up wandering out onto the porch, looking out at the darkening sky. "They weren't planning to stop for a picnic anywhere near here," I said after a while. "Was it really a tiger?"

Duncan put an arm around my shoulders. "Carol's spring was the right size. I had the right tools — new ones, too — for that engine trouble." He gently pulled me till I leaned back against his chest and rested his chin on top of my head.

"How come if I told Kim your computer was down, it was Janice who gave me the disc drive?" My eyes were beginning to adjust to the darkness. "She wouldn't even come inside to use the bathroom. Do you think they were scared our house was bugged, or something?"

"All telephones lines can be used to listen in," Duncan reminded me. "We researched that years ago. Someone probably knew they were here almost as soon as we did."

"I bet they were going somewhere, and planned to stop here. Where were they running to — or from?" We were both quiet for a while, and I could hear frogs in the long grass by the slough. "We had all these little details, and didn't put them together until now ... Well, we're on somebody's list now, that's for sure."

"Probably have been for years," Duncan said cheerfully. "With a file that reads '*Mostly harmless*.'"

It was cooler now, and I shivered. "Is that the northern lights, this late in the season?"

Duncan didn't need to look twice at the blur of light staining the southern skyline. "No," he said quietly. "That's the city lights in Edmonton." Fifty miles away, all detail of the city lights was lost in the glow that smeared out the stars above our windbreak trees.

With a Screwdriver

Dear Grandma:
You won't have heard much about all of what happened, I know, because Mom won't have told you. There are things she just thinks are not proper to talk about, especially with me or concerning me. Maybe she's a bit less straitjacketed into proper behaviour with you than she is with me, but I wouldn't bet on it. How she ever taught Leif and me that being human meant being more practical than a monkey with a screwdriver, I don't know.

So you probably haven't heard more about what happened than the short note I sent you just after. I know, I've written since then, but those letters were busy work, full of what's been happening since. There's been a lot of day-to-day stuff keeping me and Terence busy, and it's been enough to think about and to write about for you. Now that I've got a little time to myself each day to be just Laney and nothing else, I've got more time to think and write and maybe even think and write seriously to you about what happened.

And don't let Mom tell you it had anything to do with living crowded together. She's been fussing over Leif and I since we were kids. There's plenty of room in this big house, and it's because we live in a collective things were able to turn out as well as they did.

Living in the house together, even from the first day, didn't seem like being roommates; it was more like one of those small four-plex apartments built during the fifties, or living in a small village at the end of our lane. It was like walking about on campus with bright, young undergrads bubbling over their books, and truly absent-minded professors walking through a room or a crowd without seeing a thing, intent on their own thoughts. There were even artists – bright and intense people, younger and older, who had stencilled every riser in the staircase with ivy leaves and painted every rung in the handrail with a different colour from their eclectic palettes. They were the reason why the cupboards held 37 different mugs, no more than two alike, and why dinners together were simple but brought everyone out of our rooms as the good cooking odours wafted upstairs and down. It was crowded only when we had visitors in for a party.

So it's been almost a year now, and high time I did so. But I can't jump into this story with both feet, not without making sure sure you remember what I've told you before about where we live, in this city you've never seen.

When Leif and his wife Tanya found this old house for a song, they knew I'd been accepted at the University and Terence and I would be moving to town. It was even easier to buy this house together – brother, sister and spouses – than we'd hoped it would be. Maybe we all have complementary skills and interests instead of fighting over whose turn it is to cook dinner or mow the lawn. Having separate bathrooms definitely helps, and the laundry room in the basement has a john and sink for Mike.

Mike's been living here almost since we moved in. His tiny bedroom and his studio room are in the basement, and we invade his territory to do laundry or work on the furnace. That furnace has been nothing but a pain since we bought the place! It's a good thing that Mike lives here, not only since his rent helps with the mortgage, but if he weren't in the basement it would get filled up with boxes and science experiments, for sure.

There's room for only one car in the driveway, but Mike has a bus pass and Terence and I ride our bikes most places, so there's only Tanya's little Toyota parked there. When our friends come to town, they park their van in the lane. It's quiet, for all that the main drag, a block away, has traffic running twenty-four hours a day.

We do like quiet places, and that's why after a busy week on campus or on construction sites Terence and I head out to the lake with the whole household. They've had enough of work and city crowds. Tanya swears she's going to quit working at the convenience store if the theatre company ever gets that Arts grant and can pay her set designer's wages. Leif doesn't exactly enjoy working at the hotel, but he says any job that gives him time to work on his PhD is a good job.

Mom said once that it sounded like we were spending all our time together, but we're all doing different things most of the time. Carpooling for an evening to hike and swim at the lake, then home to cook a potluck dinner together doesn't crowd us too much.

One time last summer Tanya slipped on the raft and lost her keys, so while the rest of us swam, Leif worked on breaking into her car. Eventually he came back to the lakeshore with a couple of big magnets and some rope from the back of the Toyota. "Wanna go fishing for car keys?" he said with a grin. We found three sets of keys, including Tanya's, and some coins. So it became a regular thing to go fishing with the magnets. We found about $70 in change over the summer, and a couple more sets of keys, most of which got back to their owners at last.

So when our friend Adam came to town job-hunting and camped out at our place, he joined the expeditions to the lake, and became an expert magnet fisher. He could string out a story or tell jokes while hauling in coils of wet rope, and never get a drop on his clothes or miss a beat in his steady flow of words. After a couple of weeks I really came to admire his storytelling, and was thinking about it one afternoon when I went to pick him up in Tanya's Toyota when he was finished downtown.

"So what's The Resume Ranch doing open on a Sunday?" I asked as he tossed his clipboard in the back and got in.

"Special networking session for people willing to teach ESL overseas," Adam replied. He swung the door shut with a grunt. "Who was riding here last?" he asked, groping under the seat for the latch to send it sliding back a few notches.

"I was," I said, amused. The Sunday traffic was light as I headed us out toward the lake.

"Geez, were you riding with your knees up around your head?" he griped. "There's no room!"

"Mike was in the back, so I ran the seat forward to give him leg room. I had enough room."

Tugging at the seat belt, Adam said mildly, "I still don't fit."

"Well, you are twice my size," I pointed out.

"Not nearly. I'm not nearly two hundred pounds yet, even with this gut." He slapped his waistline, soft over a core of muscle.

"And I'm ... um, a hundred and twenty-mumble."

Adam shrugged. "I'm nowhere near as big as your brother, or Terence. Or Mike. Nobody's as big as Mike."

"Yeah, but he's limber. You're about as big as my guy." I thought for a moment. "What is it with this circle of people? All the men are big."

"And all the women are small? Sexual dimorphism," was Adam's reply.

"Nah, only me and your girlfriend Elly. But boy, is that ever dimorphism. Makes me feel like those sea lions where the males are four times the mass of the females."

"Even that's not the most extreme dimorphism in the animal world." Adam had shifted to his story-telling and lecturing mode. "There's a species of spider in Great Britain which ..." This interesting topic carried us all the way to the lake, where we found the other vehicle and some of us went off to hike, others to swim.

Fishing with the magnets brought in about five dollars in dimes and quarters before one of the ropes untied and we had to fish for the magnet. By then we were getting hungry, and headed to the house to cook dinner.

Adam cooked up a storm for the rest of us. He accepted help only for peeling potatoes and making the salad, doing the sauces and the entree and the vegetables himself. This was his contribution to the household, anong with burning the trash and doing some yard work in the squirrel's jungle that was starting to look something like a back yard after his sporadic labours.

Since he was still looking for work, Adam couldn't pay rent. Therefore he had begun the habit of cooking like a gourmet chef for the rest of us, and telling entertaining stories over dinner. He refused to use the room set aside as a library/computer/guest room until he could pay for it, so instead he kept all his gear in the coat closet and behind the futon couch in the living room.

"You're a convenient house guest, Adam," said Leif. "Pass the gravy, please."

"It's a roux in a reduced – " Adam shut up and passed the gravyboat. "More vegetables?" He offered Terence a bowl.

Terence shuddered. "No, but is there more meat?" He took two slices. "You've got to be at least as good a tenant as Mike. You cook better, for sure."

"We hardly know when either of them's here," said Tanya. "Unless we're having dinner like this, I mean."

"Anybody handy with a screwdriver or paintbrush would be welcome here. And except for the rent check, you probably wouldn't know I'm around," added Mike.

"Or when the smoke detector goes off," Tanya said, and kicked him under the table. "Mike, when a fire alarm rings, people usually leave a building. They don't usually run upstairs and check under all the beds, then carry and push everybody out."

"I wouldn't have minded being carried out if I'd been overcome by smoke. But I was still making the salad!" I said with a grin. Mike had whirled upstairs, checked the bedrooms and come down to catch me up in one of his great arms before I knew what was happening. He pushed Adam out the kitchen door before either of us could explain that the smoke detector had gone off because of something burning in the oven.

"You're just lucky you didn't bump into her salad knife," Tanya insisted. "You could have been cut, a couple of stitches, and you'll miss that deadline for Maple Leaf Comics. Or you could have run her into somebody else. Then we'd be making phone calls." She mimed holding an imaginary phone. "Hello, Terry won't be at the construction site today. He had a run-in with a cooking knife. No, he wasn't cooking. His wife was holding it, and a comics artist was holding his wife, and they ran into Terry. No, it wasn't art. It wasn't comic, either. It was an accident!" By this time we were laughing into the gravy.

"You can't run into Tanya either, she has to help her sister move tomorrow and then work the 3 to 11 shift at the store," Leif joined in. "Neither her sister nor her boss will like it if you phone with that kind of excuse."

"No phone calls!" Adam said over our laughter. "I'm expecting a call-back!" That set us all off again.

"Which call-back is that?" Leif fed him the straight line.

"The one with the job. You know, the job that'll make me rich and famous and powerful and the object of envy." Adam let the sarcastic groans subside. "I could end up working in Terry's construction site," he suggested, just to see my husband blanch. The thought of Adam working with power tools or moving lumber and bricks around did not inspire confidence. We had watched him clearing brush in the squirrel's jungle of our backyard. "Or I could do housekeeping at the hotel. Leif would put in a good word for me with the manager, wouldn't you?"

"Once you began changing beds in there, you'd have all the chambermaids attending seminars on 'What your union can do for you," Leif said sourly. "Management can see your type at the first interview."

"Well then, it's a good thing I have other prospects," Adam replied, undaunted. "Since I haven't been accepted either to take courses at the University or to teach them, I've pinned my hopes on becoming a stockboy at the convenience store."

Tanya laughed harder than anyone. "It does feel like that sometimes, doesn't it?" She wiped her eyes. "But you're trying hard enough that if there's work anywhere, you'll find it."

"I just want to get back into control of my life, where I have some influence and can make things happen," Adam said quietly, but I don't think most of us heard as we were clearing the table.

"Have you seen the latest Real Neat Thingamajig I got?" Leif asked Mike. "I'll go get it." He ran upstairs to the library, and brought down a small box to sit on the table. One by one, during the next few minutes, each of us wandered away from doing the dishes, or getting out a bucket of ice cream and dessert bowls, to look at it while Leif was talking.

It was a black box with a glass lid, sitting on a thick, heavy base. It was small enough that Leif could have hidden it between his cupped hands. Inside the open box was a tiny, glowing bead that floated unsupported in space. There was an on/off switch, very stiff, on the side of the base.

"So, what is it?" asked Tanya.

Leif had the same look on his face he had as a kid when we finally got our crystal set radios to work, by running an antenna wire up a tree next to the house. "Well, there's a long and complicated name for it, and it's patented in the name of one of the people I work with at the Delaney Sciences building, but the easy way to describe it is it's a black hole."

"A what?" Mike had been about to touch the glass lid. He snatched his hands away.

"A really teeny tiny one," Leif assured him.

"That's what I like about you, Leif," Terry said dryly. "Your understanding of such complex things, and how you explain them in such clear and precise terms."

"It's a micro-black hole," he said again. "Lift the case, and see how heavy it is. About six, seven pounds by now, and the case weighs less than a pound.'

"It's not black," Mike observed, looking at the glowing bead cautiously. "It's kind of like neon."

"That's because it's absorbing the air molecules that keep leaking into the case," Leif explained. "It's suspended over an electromagnet. That's what keeps it floating, and what keeps it around for so long."

Terence was looking at it with even more suspicion than Mike. I decided to wait my turn until later; the ice cream was melting, and if this turned out to be another one of Leif's jokes I didn't want to be caught.

"What do you mean, keeps it around for so long?" asked Terry, half-serious. "Does it blow up or something?"

Tanya glared at him, but Leif waved reassurance. "This kind of black holes are forming all the time, and when they've absorbed enough mass, they just disappear. No explosion. Just poof! And they're gone. We've been making them in the lab for ages, it's just hard to keep them around long enough to learn very much from them."

"And now you've got one on our kitchen table," said Tanya.

"Yep!" Leif grinned happily. "We've been working on the case design for a while. Works like a charm."

"Be the first one on your block," said Mike.

Terry was leaning back now, so I took a closer look myself. It still looked like a glowing bead floating in the middle of a small box. Was the glass lid sealed? I thought so. My husband nudged me and took my bowl of ice cream. "Thanks, Laney. Doesn't this sound like a Portable Hole, from the Dungeons and Dragons game?"

"Stuff goes in but not out. Strictly a one-way hole," Leif pointed out. "It looks pretty weird going in, too. Air glows around the point that's the black hole, as it falls in. Water swirls. More solid things fall gradually around it, and after a few minutes distort and disappear suddenly."

"So this is the handy-dandy portable black hole. Takes up less room than a trash compacter," I suggested.

"Or a garborator," Tanya added. "But we don't have either of them, because they're – " she shoved her face close to Leif's – "NOT SAFE. They crunch things. Now you've brought a black hole home."

Mike trilled, "I told you to leave your work at the office, dear," and I smacked him.

"Are we all in danger of falling into this thing? House and all?" Tanya demanded.

"No, no," Leif protested. "It's a tiny one. It'll only absorb less than a hundred kilos mass before it disappears."

I was getting myself another bowl of ice cream. "Too bad. Too small for a good trash disposal system, I guess."

"Well, don't shake it out of the box, whatever you do. It'll eat the table, and a bite out of the floor, maybe fall into Mike's studio before it evaporates." Tanya was disgusted. "Why do you want to keep such a dangerous thing at home anyway?"

"It's not dangerous when it's handled properly.'" Leif tapped the thick base of the box. "There's enough power to run this electromagnet for a month. I just brought it home to show everyone. I'll take it back when I go in to teach Tuesday."

Mike got up, shaking his head. "Nice try, Leif. Joke? No? Well, do me a favour and move it out of the kitchen. Like, say, over to the coffee table? Anywhere not over my bedroom or art table," he suggested, drawing another laugh for his paranoia. "I've got my drawings set out there and a deadline to meet. Let it eat the floor and fall into the washing machine, that'd be okay."

"If it ate the futon couch first, it might not eat the washing machine," Terry suggested. "That's got to weigh a lot, like maybe fifty kilos or a hundred and some pounds."

"You guys are sick, playing with a black hole." I left the table. "Tanya's right. What do you want to have something that dangerous around for, especially at home?"

"It isn't any more dangerous than a gun, or a kitchen knife," was Leif's answer. "Inside the case, it's safer than a knife, which you can bump against and cut yourself. The lid seals, see? It keeps out much of the air, doesn't let it get a draft started so the hole lasts a long time, compared with a few minutes, which used to be all we could get."

Terry noticed Adam leaving the room with a heaping bowl of ice cream. "Not very interested, Adam?"

"Can I get a job making or selling the things?" Adam asked around a mouthful of Maple Walnut ice cream and caramel sauce.

Leif looked doubtful. "Um ... not likely. You can ask at the Department if you want, but it's a long shot."

Adam shrugged. "I'd better try calling tomorrow. I've called everywhere else." He went to sit on the couch in the living room.

"Geez, he really is down about his job search," Terry said quietly. To cheer Adam up some, we put on a video of his favourite tv series and and heckled the screen for the next hour. I don't think any of us had any idea just how bad Adam felt.

I got a much clearer idea the next morning, when Adam began making a series of calls from the phone by the couch. Anyone walking past the living room to get breakfast got ignored while he took notes furiously on his clipboard, flipping back to earlier notes and ahead to blank pages. By the time Tanya went to drop Leif off at the hotel and help her sister move, and Terry's ride honked at the end of the driveway to take him to the construction site, Adam had the phone book and the Yellow Pages marked in half-a-dozen places each.

"Is anyone likely to be taking calls at eight a.m.?" I asked as I put a mug of chamomile tea down on the Yellow Pages. He was already too jazzed up for coffee; he needed to slow down for a while.

"I'm leaving messages on their voice mail and answering machines," he said absently, still making notes to himself. Then he looked up at me. "Don't you have classes this morning?"

"I'll be a little late getting there. First I'm giving this second breakfast a chance to stay down," I told him. I was also going to use the Pregnancy Test Kit that Terry picked up for me on the weekend, but I didn't see any reason to tell him or the rest of our housemates that yet.

Adam didn't seem to get any hint about those thoughts just from my morning nausea. He didn't seem aware of anything outside his own increasing distress and excitement. "That's it then," he said after a few more minutes of phoning. He came into the kitchen where I was drinking tea in an effort to produce a sample for the Test Kit which was still hiding in its box upstairs in my underwear drawer. Adam put his empty mug and his clipboard on the table. "I've left messages with everybody. Now it's time to wait for the call-back."

"The call-back? A particular one?"

"The one for the job that'll make me rich and famous and powerful and the object of envy." Adam stretched and yawned. His shirt hung oddly at the waist, and one of his pockets bulged.

"Got the answering machine on in case the phone rings while you're in the john?" I teased. He blanched and tripped over his own feet, running to check. "Adam! That was a joke! Chill out!" I followed him into the living room, put the woven cotton rug back in front of the fireplace and straightened the quilt he'd knocked off the old armchair. "You have got to get back in control of yourself."

"Back in control," he agreed, patting the answering machine on its glowing LED under the POWER ON switch. "You're absolutely right, I have to get back in control. Do you know what controls people? Do you know what controls men? The endocrine system alone is fascinating ..." As he spoke, Adam sat me down on the futon couch and himself on the armchair, and began to lecture me on hormone systems. It was pretty interesting stuff, and I figured if I listened for a while he would start to calm down.

Instead he got more intense, like Mike half-way through a painting with a deadline the next morning. After a while he seemed to be reaching the po int of all his explanations. "You'd think behaviour and experience would have an influence on the systems of the body which are our chemical controls, and they do," he assured me, hands gesturing wildly. "But in fact, the systems themselves send out messages which control our behaviour and how we experience what is happening."

He was waiting for a response or a question of some kind, so I fed him one. "You mean, one person will get upset by something but another will have the same thing happen and not get bothered by it?"

"Exactly! Or one person will figure it's an ordinary day, there's ordinary things going on, just get things done as usual, and another will get a random surge of testosterone or serontonin or – or – " He was waving his arms now, and turning red. "And then his behaviour will change because of the chemical environment his body makes for his mind! Driving him to fight, or to tears, or to screw! Any of the hardwired drives."

He needed to calm down. "Uh, you want a cup of tea, Adam? Before I get ready to go to class?"

"What? No ... I've got to get back into control," he said absently. "Where's my clipboard?"

"You left it on the table." I started to get up, but he waved me back.

"I'll get it," he said quickly. "You wait there, in case the phone rings." He darted into the other room and back.

"Adam, it wouldn't have time to ring twice. And the answering machine is on," I pointed out, and he nodded.

"But I've got to feel in control," he said. "You know that? Do you understand? It's not the same if it rings and I'm – " The phone rang, and both of us nearly leapt out of our skins. "I'll get it!" Adam shrieked. He closed his eyes, took two deep breaths, and picked up the receiver. "Hello, this is Adam Bentley – oh, hi, Elly. No, nothing's wrong. Look, I'm expecting a call. Yes, come over. You can help me get back in control while I wait. Bye." He hung up abruptly.

Good. He wasn't in any kind of state to leave alone, but if Elly was coming over soon, I could head out to class without worrying about his weird mood. I headed for the stairs, but he stopped me with a hand on my arm.

"Where are you going?"

"To get ready for class," I said, startled. "I'm late already."

"But I'm not finished yet," Adam protested. "Laney, you're helping me get back in control."

"No, really, I have to get my bookbag and leave – "

"No! I'm telling you, these are things people do. In other cultures, there are meditation rituals, or festivals, or chants that people do, to control their bodies and their minds." Adam was steering me towards the couch again, and took up his seat again on the chair. "People use biofeedback in attempts to control the deep, unconscious rhythms of the body. But they don't understand the unconscious rhythms of the body are speaking in everything they choose to do and – "

"Adam," I said clearly, and he stopped in mid-syllable. "I have to leave now."

"You can't leave now," he protested. "Not when I'm starting to be in control. I'm sorry, but setting the fires in the back yard isn't enough anymore. There aren't any more Band-aids in the house, not even in Mike's bathroom in the basement. And there are hardly any squirrels left around here."

"Huh?" was all that came out of my mouth. This wasn't job anxiety, this was something truly alarming.

"And it doesn't work very well with squirrels," he explained, patting my knee. "They can't listen, or talk, and they stop moving after a while.

Sure, it doesn't take long, and I can get back to work – to looking for work," he added bitterly. "But I've got time now, and have to wait for the call-back, so there's no point in looking for another squirrel. I haven't found one in the yard in a while, anyway."

"What do you want the – " I bit my tongue. There was no way I wanted to hear that question answered. "If you need some Band-aids, Adam, I'll go buy you some. We can walk down to the drugstore together," I suggested.

"No, I'm managing just fine without them," he assured me. "We're not going anywhere, you and I are just going to sit here and wait for the call-back and talk."

"I don't want to talk any more," I said as reasonably as I could. "I have to – "

"Then I'll talk. You listen." And he did talk, more of the same general topics as before, quietly enough to calm me a little. Not paying attention to what he said after a while, I wondered if getting Mike to leave his basement studio would be a good idea. Maybe the two of us could persuade Adam to go to bed for a week and just rest. Or maybe one of us could keep him talking while the other made him an appointment with a psychologist.

Adam talked for an endless time, until my patience was exhausted. "Adam," I said eventually, and he paused. "Excuse me. I have to go to the bathroom." He leaned back in the armchair, out of my personal space, and immediately I got up and headed for the stairs.

"Where do you think you're going?"

"Bathroom," I answered, surprised. "Like I said."

He shook his head. "No no no. The one just off the living room, here."

"But that's Leif and Tanya's, Terry and I use the one upstairs," I protested.

Steering me towards this floor's bathroom, Adam was insistent. "I'm not getting out of reach of the phone. And I'm not losing my train of thought. I was telling you about creative visualization and how it works both ways. Go on," he added, standing in the open doorway of the tiny room. You could wash your hands while sitting on the john, and there was hardly room for a towel bar. "I won't lose track. Creative visualization isn't only when you decide to imagine yourself getting well from cancer. It also works the other way."

I tried to push the door shut, but Adam was rooted firmly. Suddenly every difference in our sizes, weights and strength became very clear to me, and I stopped pushing. "No, Adam, I want privacy," I said, trying not to bristle or shrink under his calm gaze. His waistline didn't look so soft today, bulging where his shirt was tucked into his brown pants.

"No, Laney, I'm getting back in control," he said. Looking at his watch, he added: "I shouldn't be away from the phone much longer. If you need to, you should go now. You won't get a chance to later, I'll be busy." He did look away then, towards the phone and its little red light. "Creative visualization doesn't only happen when you're imagining yourself well. As you become ill, for example as tumors grow, the body can sense its own unwellness and influence your dreams and waking visions with images which show, in retrospect, that your body can be aware of its own illnesses and tell the conscious mind long before a formal diagnosis."

So much for taking a sample for the Pregnancy Test Kit upstairs. I didn't need it now, anyway. I was completely sure now, not only that I was pregnant, but that what was happening to Adam could not be fixed with a week of chicken soup and comic books in bed.

Adam didn't want any more conversation from me after that. Content to let me return to sit on one end of the futon couch, he gave me the benefit of his research and opinions without seeming to notice that my attention was elsewhere.

A knock came at the front door, and the door opened. Elly leaned her head inside. "Hello, anybody home? Adam, you here?"

"Elly, we're out of milk here. Let's go get some for tea," I said, as Adam looked at the phone and the door and back at the phone. I stood up, but Adam put a hand on my chest and pushed me effortlessly back onto the couch.

"No. Turn the deadbolt, Elly," he said. "We're not going out."

"Then ask Mike to bring up his cream, or canned milk," I told Elly, as she came into the living room, still wearing her coat and shoes; but as I spoke Adam took Elly by the hand, kissed her absently and sat her on the couch beside me.

"Don't call Mike. We're going to stay right here while I get back in control. Until I get my call-back. The right one, for the right job for me," Adam said. He held Elly's hand. "We'll just talk, nobody else. Stay away from the phone," he said to me in the same quiet, thoughtful tone. "I'll answer if it rings. Don't make any calls."

When I tensed to beat my feet and fists on the floor, he noticed, and put out a hand to stop me. "Don't do that," he said, still quiet. "Don't bang on the floor and bring Mike up here. I'll break her arm and snap your neck before he gets here. And I can control him, too." He put one hand into his pants pocket, smiled, and took it out again. "We don't need any fires, or squirrels. I'll do fine with what's here."

I didn't have much chance to get to know Elly well in the last couple of weeks. She was sweet-tempered and quiet, I knew. Now I gave her credit for intelligence as she figured out what was happening much faster than I had. She didn't say anything at first, just looked at me sitting beside her. I didn't have any plan to signal to her, no weapon or nerve gas ready to hand, of course. Unless she had a dart gun in her coat pocket I didn't have any idea of what we could do as Adam began lecturing again.

Having an audience of two seemed to inspire Adam and he held forth quite eloquently on fakirs and shamans for a while. I couldn't remember a word he said as soon as it was out of his mouth. All I could think was that there were two of us here now, and Adam didn't calm down any more for Elly than he did earlier. She suggested he might like a cup of coffee, and brought a hand-rolled cigarette out of her belt pouch, but he turned down both offers firmly.

It was the phone that interrupted his lecture, not Elly. "I'll get it!" Adam shrieked, exactly on pitch with the shrill ring. He closed his eyes, breathed deeply twice, and picked up. As he spoke into the receiver, Elly and I shared another glance, trying to relax.

"This been going on long?" she asked.

"Since about eight this morning. He only started to scare me for real about an hour ago." I was trembling very slightly, almost invisibly. "Got any ideas?"

She glanced significantly at her belt pouch. "I should make us some tea," she began, but clearly didn't want to say more with Adam chatting brightly on the phone two feet away. She passed me the hand-rolled cigarette. "In case you make it," she said briskly while Adam took notes on his clipboard. When Elly shifted her weight he took hold of her hand again to prevent her getting up, still scribbling notes.

I knew what must be in the cigarette, but didn't think we'd get it into him. "Adam, we're leaving now," I said loudly, and headed for the door.

Elly's sudden intake of breath came as Adam said good-bye and hung up. "No, you'll get back here," he said behind me. I didn't even have the deadbolt turned before he came to usher me back to the living room, drawing Elly along with him by the hand. "I don't want to say it again and again, I don't want to hurt either of you. I just want to get back in control. Both of you are going to stay here with me till I get my call-back." He pushed us toward the couch again.

"I don't like this, Adam," Elly said, rubbing her hand. "Stop, you're hurting me."

"That isn't the point this time," he said absently, and reached for his clipboard to look at his notes again.

Speaking firmly and confidently didn't seem to be getting much results, but I tried again. "Elly and I want to leave now. Let us go."

"No no no. You're staying till I get the right call-back."

"Wasn't that a call-back?" I asked.

"It wasn't the right one," he explained. "They're not hiring for a couple of weeks. I need work right away."

"I'm sorry it wasn't the right one, but you can't just keep at us like this," I told him.

"Yes, I can. I'm getting back in control. It doesn't matter that this wasn't the right call. I can control other things," he said cheerfully. "Elly! You haven't even taken off your coat or shoes yet. You'd better do it now."

She was still rubbing her hand. "Why?"

"Because I say so," he said pleasantly. "Now. Up and at 'em! Can't wear shoes on the hardwood floors."

Elly got out of her shoes and coat while I thought miserably that I didn't care how many hours Terry and I had spent sanding and refinishing the floors. We could tap-dance in hob-nailed boots for all I cared, so long as we were heading out the door where we could find more people to help us deal with Adam. I didn't think the two of us had much chance of locking him in the bathroom or getting knives from the kitchen to defend ourselves. He was appallingly strong.

"Hmm," he said when she put her duffle coat down. "Not enough. Take 'em all off." Elly stared. "You heard me. Take off your clothes. You too, Laney."

"No. This is ridiculous," Elly spluttered.

"Doesn't matter. It's what I said. I'm getting in control, and this is what I want to happen," he said smugly. "Strip. Now. Both of you." Something in the way he stood changed, and he looked bigger suddenly. Harder.

"For crying out loud," I said, trying not to shiver. "You've seen me naked. We all went skinny-dipping at the lake."

Elly folded her arms across her chest. "You've certainly seen me naked. A rather close inspection, as I recall, when you gave me a full body massage last Friday," she said coldly.

"Oh, this isn't a social or a sexual thing," he added with a dismissive wave. "It's about making things happen." He loomed over us, seeming broad and tall as a closed door.

The bruises on Elly's hand were already red and welting up. It seemed unreal, but she and I did as he said, taking as long as we could about it. I even folded my jeans. I never fold my jeans. I put my t-shirt on top of my underwear. Why should I try to hide my plain cotton underwear from him? He was staring at my skin as attentively as he'd watched the video last night.

"Sorry, Laney," Elly said quietly, bare as a boiled egg. "I should have realized he was going spla."

"Hey, he's been living here." I shrugged. "I should have picked up some kind of indic—"

Adam clapped to get our attention. "I want to tell you about the names people give what drives them," he said. "The affectionate nicknames. Turn around once, yep, both of you, unh-hunh, and you can sit down and listen." This time he was trying for humour, I think, but a more appreciative audience would be a better judge of his comedy. I think his delivery suffered more than a little from wandering attention, as he inspected the goosebumps rising on Elly's arms, or my quivering knees.

He interrupted his narrative at one point to say, "Unclench your toes, Laney. That's unbecoming." How could I relax my toes? All the yoga exercises for relaxation that I'd ever learned flew straight out of my head.

The phone rang again as he was coming to an end of a tiresomely long list of nicknames for body parts. "Tom, Dick and Harry. Screwdriver. — I'll get it," he cried again, and calmed himself before picking up the phone. I was inwardly furious that he could remember how to relax even when he was having some kind of a breakdown.

Once Adam was absorbed in his phone call, Elly got up and headed for the door, but Adam caught her by the arm and pushed her back on to the couch again. "Hm," she said to me reflectively as he continued talking without missing a beat in the conversation. "This isn't too awful, so far."

"Optimist," I replied, looking at her bruises and the hand still holding her arm.

"When is anybody else due home?" she asked.

This was Monday, so I thought for a moment before answering. "Not till six o'clock, for supper." The floor under our feet shook as the basement door slammed.

"That's Mike, leaving. And if I go to the window to wave at him—"

As I began to stand, Adam's grip visibly tightened and Elly winced. I sat back, shivering, and saw his fingers loosen.

She sighed. "Bet you wish it was Will and Dana who came to visit, instead of me. The two of them could hold him while you called the cops or bashed him with a lamp."

"No lamps," I mourned. "All the sculptures are upstairs, too. Just a stupid little black box and the phone book on the coffee table. Maybe I could bash him with the answering machine."

"Well, do it now, then," she said suddenly, and screamed. "Call th—" She didn't even get two words out before Adam's big hand was over her mouth.

I snatched at the answering machine, but his other hand suddenly held both of mine against the light, cool plastic. "Sorry," he was saying smoothly into the phone receiver tucked under his ear. "I'll just turn the radio down. Those dramas get loud suddenly." I was crying ow, ow, ow as his hand tightened and he glared at me. "Thanks, then. Call you next week. Good-bye." He hung up as I cried out, shook each of us once, and let us go.

"There won't be any more of that," he said.

There wasn't anything to say in response to that. The room seemed colder, and quieter after the pages of Adam's clipboard stopped flipping. He picked it up from where it had fallen, and looked at his notes. "Well, this one wasn't any good either." He put the clipboard on the coffee table. "There'll have to be something else controlled now," he said then, looking at the goosebumps along our arms and legs and the way Elly's nipples had gone hard with cold.

"It'll be sex then," he decided.

My second breakfast churned inside me. I almost lost this toast-and-egg too. "I don't want to have sex," I said woodenly.

"And I don't want to be raped," Elly snapped.

Adam sighed. "This isn't about rape. It's about making things happen. And I want to have sex."

Sullenly, Elly muttered, "I don't want you to hurt me again. Or Laney."

"I won't hurt you," he said reasonably. "I don't want that, I want sex. One of you will probably be enough. You'll do, Elly, you know what I like."

"All right," she said suddenly. "Let's go to a bedroom, then. I don't want Laney to be around."

He shook his head. "We'll stay here, by the phone. Both of you get up and unfold the couch out into a bed. There's a screwdriver behind the couch, to loosen the big screws." I hadn't known it was there. While unfolding the couch, I kept trying to think, but I was too numb to be any good at it. The screwdriver was too light to throw at him, and too dull to stab him with; it would only gouge and tear. Sure, that would hurt, but it wouldn't stop him.

When the couch frame was unfolded into a bed, he motioned for Elly to lie back on the sheet that had been folded inside the futon.

"Laney should go away," she said. "I don't want her here when you're doing this." She was trying to get me out of there, I realized.

But Adam was unbuttoning his long-sleeved shirt, wrapping something in it that had been tucked into his waistband. "No," he said, putting aside the shirt with a quiet thunk next to the phone. "She'll stay right here." He loosened his pants, lowered himself on top of her, and took hold of my wrist in one hand and her throat in the other. "Laney, stay right here."

It was a lucky thing that I couldn't reach the screwdriver or the phone, or even my own shoes. I didn't have to try to hit him or think about getting away. Every time I moved, his hand tightened on my wrist and I heard Elly whine no, no, no. Looking at him moving on her had about as much appeal as thinking about whatever it was Adam must have done with the squirrels, so I looked instead at his hand where it gripped my arm. His own arm was marked from wrist to elbow with thin red cuts, some a few days old and healing, others scabby and new. No wonder he'd been wearing long-sleeved shirts for the last week or so. Then I sat and thought of nothing until he got up after a while and let go of us.

Adam put his shirt back on and adjusted all his clothes, pinching the crease in his pants and settling his collar at the back of his neck. Elly's jaws worked. "I have to go to the bathroom," she said hoarsely.

He stood in the doorway for her, too, holding me by my other wrist and apologising for stepping on my bare foot. I hardly felt it at that point. Still trying to think, I must have looked withdrawn but inside my mind was a whirlwind. A whirlwind with only one coherent thought, I admit, but What To Do Now was a pretty high priority on my agenda for the day.

"I'm cold," I said while Adam ushered us back to the couch. "Both Elly and I are cold. We have to get dressed now." She was shivering now, long shudders that made her blonde braids shake.

"No, you don't have to get dressed," he muttered, looking through his notes again. After a minute he glanced up and must have seen Elly's hands trembling. "Wrap up in the sheet, Elly, that'll warm you up.

Here's the quilt from the chair for you, Laney. Be patient, and I'll talk to you again in a minute."

Wrapping up did help our shivering back down to a low-grade, occasional tremble as Adam began another of his long-winded spiels, to which I no longer even pretended to be paying attention. It also helped, obscurely, to be uncovered no longer in front of Adam in his "interview clothes", which was a very different experience from skinny-dipping at the lake with a couple of friends.

Knowing this quilt was the one Adam had slept under for the past few weeks did not endear it to me, though. Auntie's Log Cabin quilt was not going to stay a day longer in my house, that was for sure. Terry could take it to work for rags.

Getting the quilt out of the house came second after getting Adam out. A little warmer now, I could think more clearly. What would be happening if it were Terry or Mike who'd been home when Adam needed to get back in control of himself, and ended up getting in control of me and Elly? Then Adam would have taken out whatever he was hiding under his shirt, probably a handgun of some kind, and somebody would have ended up shot.

I didn't like imagining that, not even imagining Adam shot. I just wanted him straitjacketed in a rubber room somewhere right then. There had to be some other way for things to happen.

If Tanya were home, she'd still be in her and Leif's room working on set designs for the theatre company or ironing her store uniform. Adam wouldn't have gone upstairs, away from the phone. He might have set a fire in the living room, or brought in a squirrel for whatever it was he did with them, but that would be downstairs on the other side of her locked door. So she would have been okay. All I had done when Adam first looked distressed was give him chamomile tea and let myself be pushed around.

I didn't know what else was practical to do. My guy Terry never pushed me around. Leif had never pushed me around when we were kids. He'd always been the big brother with the science projects set up in his room, who made our intercoms and crystal sets and always had time to help me set up my telescope and learn to read star maps. He knew something about almost everything, and how to talk about it.

Briefly I tuned into Adam's droning lecture. This time his theme was invaders raping and pillaging, and how the next generation of people is stronger becaue of hybrid vigour. Elly leaned against me, warm against my shoulder and thigh, huddled in the sheet. I thought about my brother again.

Leif would have turned Adam's first lecture into a conversation, and would never have let Adam take control of what was happening. If necessary, Leif would have distracted him with an M.C. Escher drawing or a new electronic toy or gizmo, and jumped out a window after saying there was another Real Neat Thingamajig in the next room.

"I want a cup of tea," Elly said, through chattering teeth. "I want a cup of orange pekoe tea like my grandma makes, with lots of milk and sugar. I've got tea and some pouches of turbinado sugar in my belt pouch. I'm going to make us some tea," she said, but she hesitated to stand up under Adam's sudden glare.

"I was talking," he said. "Don't interrupt me. You're not going to be allowed in the kitchen."

"Then let Laney make us a cup of tea," she pleaded. "I'm still cold and I'm hungry and thirsty. It would be really nice if you tell her to do that. Maybe you want a sandwich or something."

Adam dismissed her ideas with a wave of his hand. "Nobody needs any of that. I think—" He was interrupted by the phone's strident ring, and we were treated to his panic and relaxation ritual again before he answered it. He had to turn away in his chair to let more light fall on his clipboard from the window; the light was changing as the day dragged on to afternoon.

Almost inaudibly, Elly mumbled to me: "There's more grass and my valium in my belt pouch, but he won't let me get anything to slip it to him."

"I've still got your cigarette thing." It was mashed up and sweat-soaked in my left fist. "But he won't let me, either."

Cursing softly, Elly sagged a little more against me. "I'm about fresh out of ideas," she admitted.

"So am I."

"If worse comes to worst, I'll — I'll wrap myself around him and try to slow him down long enough for you to get out the door and scream," she suggested. Her voice wobbled a bit. "Just keep running."

I'd have to keep running, because if he caught me he'd hurt me too. The thought banished any sense of warmth the quilt gave.

Adam was saying good-bye and hanging up, and he didn't look as if there had been good news. "That's that," he said briskly and he put the clipboard down neatly beside the phone. "That was the one I really wanted and it didn't pan out, so I'm going to have to keep control over something else." He thought for a minute.

"I'm really sorry," he said at last. "But I'm afraid there's going to be some scraping and bruising now. Maybe some cutting and bleeding."

My ears started to ring, and there were spots in front of my eyes as Adam ran his hands through his auburn hair, making it stand out in spikes. He said crossly, "Oh, don't go all green like that, Laney. It's none of that sordid sex stuff you didn't want to watch. It'll all be very clinical and impersonal, like being examined in a doctor's office. We'll have you stretched out on the coffee table here — a little bit of a thing like you should fit on it nicely — and it'll be like getting your teeth checked or having a Pap smear. Clear those things off the coffee table," he said, indicating it with a wave. "Take off the quilt, and oh, hand me the screwdriver."

Elly stiffened. "Adam, stop this."

The light was fading; it was really afternoon and there were still spots in front of my eyes. "No, I won't stop, Elly," was his mild reply. "This isn't about consent, and trust. This is about control. And this is what I want to control. I want it to be enough. I don't want to have to kill both of you, it's hard enough to bury the squirrels. Laney, clear the table now." His voice got harder, and he looked bigger and harder again.

I watched my hands put the phone book on the floor, and take the screwdriver in one hand and the little black box in the other. Somewhere in the back of my mind I was trying to remember something as the phone rang again.

Adam snatched up the receiver without even pausing to breathe, and I stood there flat-footed. What was I holding? A screwdriver that I'd damned well stick up his nose rather than just blithely hand over for him to gouge at me. And the little black box, Leif's latest Real Neat Thingamajig that he'd shown us last night. It was surprisingly heavy in my hand, about eight pounds. Maybe it was heavy enough to bash Adam over the head, if he'd let me near enough.

I looked at the box. Under the glass cover was a glowing bead, suspended in the middle of the box. If this really was a black hole ... The glowing bead was vibrating rhythmically, in time with my trembling, as if it were a ball-bearing sitting on one of the magnets we went fishing with, for lost keys in the lake. My fingers found the on-off switch on the side of the base.

On the couch, Elly had pulled an end of the sheet over her head and face. There was no hope in her huddled, muffled shape. Adam was talking brightly and animatedly on the phone, turned away from me so the light from the window could fall on his clipboard page. Then my heart pounded, and I could see clearly.

With the screwdriver I pried the sealed glass lid off the case. The bead glowed brighter in that instant. I swung the box towards Adam, across the couple of feet separating us, thinking to myself, "It's heavier than a softball. Aim for the back of his neck, it'll fall lower." And as my arm reached the top of a careful swing, my hand flicked the electromagnet's switch to OFF and let go of the box.

The bead hit him first, about half-way down his back and to one side, just as Adam was saying into the phone, "Yes, I can make the flight this afternoon." He winced as the box hit him almost in the same moment. I had seen the bead disappear as it touched him ... but what did that mean? There was a tiny hole with clean edges in the back of Adam's shirt as he turned round to take hold of my hand. Almost absent-mindedly, he held onto me as he finished his call. "The ticket will be waiting at the airport? I'll call a cab and be there," he said with confidence. "I've got everything under control and I can leave in a moment."

He hung up and slammed his clipboard shut. My pulse pounded so hard, I was sure he could feel it against his hand. "That was it! That was the call-back I've been waiting for," he crowed. "Not the best job I applied on, but these people want me today. I was here to take the call when they needed someone."

Letting go of me, he darted past the neat piles of Elly's and my clothing and over to the coat closet. "Laney, don't throw things at me," Adam added over his shoulder as he threw open the closet door, pulled out his suitcase and found his shoes next to Terry's winter boots and Tanya's sneakers. "That was the single most important phone call of my life. You're lucky you didn't really interfere with it." He struggled into his shoes and dragged his suitcase back to the armchair where he'd left his clipboard. "I am just too busy to bother with you right now," he muttered as he took something from his pants pocket, an quickly put it into the suitcase. Then he picked up the phone and dialed a number scrawled on the front page of his clipboard.

"Cab At The Curb," said a crisp female voice out of the phone while I stood tense and alert. Adam gave her the address, and I heard her say pleasantly: "We've just dropped someone off in your neighbourhood. You'll see our car out front in a few moments. Have a nice day," she chirped. Elly straightened from her huddled pose, and I noticed that the sheet had slipped off her head. She looked at me suddenly in warning, and my heartbeat accelerated even more.

Hanging up, Adam reached for his clipboard and put it on top of his suitcase. "Passport here. Bank card and emergency cash, unh-hunh. I'm going overseas to teach English," he said for our benefit. "Last-minute replacement. I've hardly got time to deal with both of you. And certainly not properly. I usually buried the squirrels, after all. But nobody else is due home for hours, and there isn't any extradition treaty where I'm going," he said cheerfully. "So I don't need to worry about that."

"You don't need to worry about that anyways," I told him. "We're not like the squirrels. You don't have to—"

"Oh, but you can talk," he said impatiently.

"You can't tell squirrels not to talk, but you can tell us," I suggested. "And you know we won't talk. We've done everything else you said."

I could see him mulling the idea over. "You did, didn't you both?" he said thoughtfully. That seemed to please him.

Elly stirred. "Because you are in control, Adam," she said.

At that moment a car horn honked outside. Adam swelled with confidence this time, instead of malice. "Very well then," he said. "Neither of you will ever tell anyone about this. I'm telling you and that's what I want to happen." He waited till he saw Elly and I each nod, numbly. "All right then. I'm off to the airport and my job which will make me rich and famous and powerful and the object of envy — at least where I'll be living."

Picking up his suitcase and clipboard, Adam grabbed his jacket from the closet, unlocked the door, and ran out to the waiting cab. He didn't even bother closing the door behind him.

I padded, barefoot, up to the front door, closed it and locked it. "Let's call 911," I said to Elly as I came back to the living room with the quilt dragging behind me.

She already had the phone in her hand. "What about using the auto-redial button so we can get the cab company to warn their driver about this passenger headed to the airport?"

"Whatever you think is best," I agreed, and she grinned.

We had time to make both calls, get dressed and eat all the leftovers in the fridge, plus a pot of coffee, before the cops arrived. Terry left work when we called and came home — I'm still not sure how he got here — and Leif left a chambermaid at the hotel front desk. If he spent Mondays on campus, we'd never have been able to reach him in the lab. Everybody else heard about what happened later, when they came home or as I was able to phone them while writing out my statement.

The police kept trying to reassure us, even though they never did find Adam. They knew he'd been in the cab. The driver talked to him as they got in and turned onto the main road headed for the airport. But over the highway traffic noises the driver heard some kind of funny sound, and looked back. Adam wasn't there anymore.

The police told us Adam jumped out of the moving cab (at highway speed, yet) and is on the run. He left behind his passport, money and the plane ticket waiting for him at the airport. The police said that suggests he doesn't want any connection with his past, and he won't come back.

It was Leif who pointed out that evening, that the clipboard was also found in the cab. "Adam always kept that clipboard with him, on some kind of emotional umbilical cord, since I've known him." Leif turned the empty black box over and over in his hands at the kitchen table, while Mike made dinner for the rest of us and we waited for Tanya to finish her shift at eleven. "Carrying dead squirrels around in his suitcase is a new thing, though. I'm sorry we didn't know he was going weird like that."

"What did you tell the cops you threw at him?" Mike asked, stirring a pot of mushroom soup at the stove.

"I told them I threw the black box at him."

Mike nodded slowly. "And what did you tell Elly to say?"

"I wasn't about to tell Elly to do anything!" I snapped. "When she heard me say that to the police, she said she had the sheet over her head then and didn't see anything."

"She said she did." Terry came to stand behind my chair at the table and rubbed my shoulders. "What did she see?"

His hands felt good. "Before the cops got here, she asked me what I threw at him so carefully. I told her it was my brother's miniature black hole." I giggled. "She said, 'Cool. Nice to have an event horizon for this whole crummy event.' Gee, I hope her parents don't give her a hard time tonight, looking after her."

"People who love you always drive you bats, but that's usually okay." Mike threw chopped onions into a big frying pan of hash browns, and wiped his hands. "So what happened to Adam? Leif, was it a real black hole?" he asked.

Leif left the table. "It was supposed to be interesting, and funny, like a joke." He left the room, and we heard his footsteps going upstairs to his room, where he stayed till Tanya came home.

There isn't any more to tell you, Grandma, and I have to get back to the baby. Tanya only babysits for an hour before she goes to work. Little Eric does take up most of my time, and he's the reason why my letters to you have been so short for most of the last year. And why my notes have been full of descriptions of him, from his beautiful toenails to his curling red hair.

Anyone who sees those red curls and knew Adam jumps to conclusions, but Terry at least believed me when I said that Adam had sex only with Elly, not me. And I keep the album of old family pictures in the living room now, with pictures of you and Granddad and your brother who died in the War, red-haired Jimmy. I looked at those pictures often during the last year, thinking of good memories, and went to the lake often, and wrote you cheerful notes instead of dwelling on what happened when Adam fell apart. I was busy making a baby, and a positive attitude gets me through the easy days as well as the difficult ones, even now.

I've got to run. Enjoy your bingo, Grandma.

Love, Laney.

Smoke and Bubbles Rising

I remember smoke rising up into the clear sky, into the baking hot blue day; and the barbecues firing up behind the houses out of sight from the road traffic, with the burnt offerings sending up a heavenly scent up to the deep bowl of blue sky.

I come round a door and there are people there already, friends, all taller than I am, looking down to see me. For a while there is a hand on my shoulder, a hug from one and a half-hug from another as we talk in murmurs, not real talking, not about real things, not about what we all know and what we all are thinking.

It's odd to see blank faces, carefully blank faces instead of cheerful chatter and the interplay of smiles. Indoors, outdoors in shade or shadow the faces aren't lighting up. Oh, two faces look the same as always. My parents are busy, same as always.

Out on the patio, my father has the barbecue lit up already and, with a spatula in one lean hand, he is turning meat on the grill. He drinks from the beer bottle in his other hand, the bottle tipping up to drain, amber glass up in an arc against the blue bowl of the sky. Blue eyes wide as he grins, he is happy as he always is when the doors are open and people going in and out in the smoke from the barbecue.

Inside the house, my mother is taking potatoes baked in tin foil out of the oven, burning her long, crooked fingers through the folded tea towel. She is as happy as she ever gets, as her pursed mouth ever looks after cutting the meat, wrapping and baking the potatoes, making the salad, mixing the Koolaid, slicing and buttering the garlic bread, and getting the cutlery and plastic plates and glasses and condiments all outside onto the old table beside the picnic blankets. She is happy enough, if I asked her she'd say so. But she doesn't look it, even when she drains her glass of beer, leaving a ring of foam.

"It's easier this way," says my father, turning the meat. "Simpler. No fussing." My mother passes him with a stack of paper napkins and an ashtray and her cigarettes. "We didn't plan this. No, that would change the way we live. Completely. This is better."

Empty faces, not saying anything, as my friends mill in and out the doors and around the yard in the smoke going up. Empty mouths, not eating yet. Empty hands, not holding or carrying anything, putting down immediately anything that's picked up. Something is happening, something I can't see, something out of sight and out of mind for those who do not know to look for it.

I don't know where to look for it and don't need to. There is something inevitable in among us, insubstantial like the smoke swirling and rising. It comes in around a corner, around a doorway, with her, with more people, more people who know. We aren't looking for it, as we meet my sister and hug her a little, not too hard, but we know.

It is here, it is near, it is a word away, a word that not one of us will say to her, not for anything, not to anyone here, least of all the two who are busy at the smoking grill and the lit cigarette and another beer each because everyone is here at last.

Everyone but one. For my parents that one is my brother-in-law, thousands of miles away at a commitment he couldn't break.

For the rest of us, we know who is not here and we cannot speak of it. I even see my brother-in-law through the smoke. He says nothing. He is too far away, of course, and doesn't know what to say. He never told me anyway, he never said anything about it then or later. But this is now and he says nothing to me, only looks down to meet my eyes and away and murmurs and moves through the smoke.

The heat from the fire comes up through the ground, burns my feet as I come towards him. Through the smoke I see him, arm's length away and out of reach, no words to say. At my feet the fire is hotter, baking the ground hard and tan. The ashes are powdery white, flaking, and the charred wood and bone blacken in the flames.

I kneel beside the fire. I have knelt beside so many fires. I have never needed to light a fire, never needed to blister these small, idle hands with anything but pastimes and luxury. I have chosen to learn this, not to be ignorant and unprepared. I don't have to be here. It could have been me.

The child looks like my son, golden hair in the ashes. He is lying half-curled in the fire, limbs twisted. He is no bigger than I am, now, and will never be any bigger. I've long known I am no bigger than a child. But to know that he will never get bigger than me, ever, breaks my heart. I've been willing to carry him, broken or bleeding or scorched, and soothe him in the little ways I know.

I kneel in the ashes and stroke the golden hair off the hot forehead. "It doesn't have to be this way," I say, and my words are one more torment for him and for any I am fool enough to let hear. We are all seared as the smoke rises up.

"Yes, it does," he says through cracked lips, with the curves of antlers burning beside his ribs. "I don't want to do any more. I'm broken. I want to be done."

I deserved that. I knew what was happening and this is my only part in it, to be here with blistering knees and hands as he burns, or not to be here at all. Some aren't here, after all, and my brother-in-law is only here in thought and memory, not spirit, for he puts no words like spirit into the flesh that is so arguably here or not here.

I can't even kiss him, either of them, one shuffling in the smoke an arm's-length out of reach and the other scorching under my hands in the flames. The coals flare under him, scent of cedar flaring up and around me as I flinch back. The blood bubbling in his ear is red, bubbles rising impossibly red, and leaking from his cracked lips blackened and caking dry.

It will be ages before he is gone, while the smoke rises up and the hiss of flames over coals mingles with the meat sizzling on the grill and the hiss of the gas flame. I sit back on a picnic blanket the colour of baked earth, hearing the sigh of bubbles rising as another beer is opened and poured for my mother and father who do not see what I see, who do not hear what I hear and who do not notice as we sit in a circle around my sister, how we keep her at the center of ourselves as we pretend to talk and pretend to eat the food for what comfort it can give us. The smoke rises up from behind our house, from other houses on the block on block of streets, smoke rising into the blue dome of the sky.

Sleep

My sleep's been interrupted for a while. There are a lot of reasons. I've been trying to relax and go with it, remembering that when you let it happen, you get the sleep you need, pretty much. I don't stew over the job, don't fret over my aging parents' health, don't try to figure out what my grown kids are doing in clubs and bars. I don't fret any more over things I can't change, like the way my late grandfather used to paint over the dents and scratches on his Buick when he'd had a wee fender-bender in a parking lot.

At least, I don't think I do. But the migraines are coming more frequently, some small and familiar, some with the intensity of the world ending about two inches behind my right ear. And some days catching the bus for work I walk like a drunk, swaying with my knapsack. So when my landlady's irregular hours mean that the front or back door could be wrenched open to let out her dogs or slammed behind them at any hour of the day or night, well, it's been interrupting my sleep where it didn't use to.

I've been taking amitriptyline. A small dose at night is pretty effective at reducing the frequency and intensity of migraines. There's less reeling and swaying when I walk, too. Another thing it does is encourage a solid night's sleep, and relief from chronic pain. Pretty nice.

When I wake up in the mornings, my usual thing has always been to open my eyes early, peer around and see the familiar room, door here, window there, then close the eyes for another drowsy few minutes before getting up. Lately the few minutes has been stretching to a half-hour.

It was hard to open my eyes this morning, and my head and limbs felt so heavy that stretching out one arm felt like doing yoga. Moving one leg took the intense concentration of doing tummy crunches. Window, still too dim for time to be awake. Both doors stood open, one wide, one a crack. I could hear my partner typing in the next room when sleep took me in a wave like pounding surf, and I drifted in suddenly deep water.

My mother-in-law came to talk to me, and I was surprisingly pleased to see her – she hadn't really liked me at all until her last year, but she was showing me a new farm now where a lot of people were visiting. In the ordinary farmhouse kitchen, she stood between the stove and the counter, then slipped aside to let other people pass. Among the faces unfamiliar to me were my father-in-law and his new wife – I'd always known what she would have thought of that, but she just said, "We don't belong here now," and took me outside to the barn.

It was a big barn, and clean, with a long row of shelves and a workbench counter. My knapsack was there and I got some clothes from it, to be warmer, but my legs still looked rather bare in silk long johns. She looked shorter than me, and I took hold of her shoulders, trying to get her to stand straight, but she was shorter than me, now.

We went outside where there were children running on the short grass, and people walking around, and glass balls rolling about on the lawn. There were a few, then dozens, and more, small like eggs and softball size and ten-pin-bowling ball size, in bright colours rolling in one direction and turning and rolling in another like a flock of birds in flight. The children ran through them, picking them up or watching them roll aside. I picked one up myself; it opened in half and another rolled out and away. Bright colours, like Christmas balls rolling and wheeling, more now. One ball had something like bunny ears, shiny purple foil fluttering. Another had bigger ears, others had bumps. There were more balls now, enough for everybody.

One ball reached up, with a hand on it, and took mine in a firm grip.

Both doors stood open, one wide, one a crack. I could hear my partner typing in the next room. I blinked and carefully rolled out of bed, onto my feet, head reeling, and walked out the door to see my partner sitting at my desk, typing.

"I saw your mother," I told him.

"And how is she?" he asked.

"She painted the car."

"Sure that wasn't your grandfather?"

"No, it wasn't him, this car looked good. She was taking me to a new farm where lots of people were visiting." I sat in his usual seat by the window and told him about the people in and around the house, and the barn and the children and the balls rolling. "I'm taller than her now."

I walked back into the bedroom and got some clothes on to be warmer, new silk long johns under my jeans. There was only one door out of the bedroom. Sometimes the other door opens a crack. I'm not going through that door again today.

Ring the bells that still can ring
Forget your perfect offering
There is a crack in everything
That's how the light gets in
– Leonard Cohen

What Scares You?

"Write what you know." That's a statement made countless times as advice to beginning writers. When you're looking to write horror, though, the advice is more properly in the form of a question: "What scares you?"

A writer can answer this question in many ways. Try exploring personal fears – "write what you know" is still good advice. Write what you know about the things that scare you. And ask the question of your characters as you are writing. It's a useful writing tool to know where the answers are different from one character to the next. These answers may not be what you outlined at the beginning of a writing project... and they may take your project in unexpectedly successful directions.

There will be some surprises. People don't always fear the same things for the same reasons. As you learn to understand the fears that people have, you can learn how to show your characters' fears, whether by inference or in bald statements.

In this chapter, I'm writing about that topic "What Scares You?" There was a panel discussion called The Future Of Monsters at a conference in Calgary, ConVersion in August 2001. That was the year I was co-editor of the Tesseracts 7 anthology. There were five topics of discussion that day, five questions about what scares the three other panellists and me, and our panel moderator. Again and again, our discussion returned to the issue of How to Write About What Scares You, as each of us panellists gave examples of published books that deal with elements of each of these topics. When I remember what we panellists said, I try not to put words in the mouths of the other writers. Each of them had such a good grasp on the craft.

The grand older man on our panel was William Sarjeant, a professor of geology who had brought real world science into an earlier panel on Extraterrestrial Cataclysms. For The Future Of Monsters panel, he changed hats and identities, and spoke as Antony Swithin. Those are his middle names, which he used as a pen name when writing his fantasy novels. The first question put to our panel of writers was "What makes a scary monster?" We gave pride of place to Bill/Antony, and let him answer this first question.

For Bill/Antony, words suggested horror far better than pictures. Horror films might sell a lot of tickets, but he'd rather read a book, or write one. Words allow a reader to visualize his or her own worst fears. A picture loses impact by comparison – it's not the reader's personal fear. Wet, messy scenes on screen cannot be as monstrous as what is not seen but only implied. He felt that applied to words in writing too; it was possible to describe a scene too thoroughly in terms of emotionally loaded material. A description that was too thorough limited what the reader could bring to the scene.

I agreed with him. We talked about something Harlan Ellison had written in The Glass Teat. Ellison had written about his own dissatisfaction with what he called "knife-kill porn" films. Ellison believes that there is bad horror writing that bears the same relationship to good writing that the scummiest pornography bears to good erotica. Some of the multitude of horror films and novels released every year are not artistic or telling a story – these "thrill kill" pieces are sloppy work. Ellison wrote of an Italian black-and-white film he had seen, in which a little girl was sent out in the evening to get a bag of flour for her mother. But there was a leopard people had seen near the village! Rubbish, the mother said, and sent the child out the door. The camera followed the girl through the village and back towards her home. She kept looking about fearfully, into the shadows as she ran. Inside the kitchen door, her mother heard the little footsteps running up to the step, and little hands beating on the door. "Mother, let me in, the leopard is coming," she cried. Rubbish, said the mother, and as she turned, there was a thump against the door. Flour sifted through all the cracks of the door, and a dark liquid trickled under it.

Now that was a proper horror scene, according to Ellison. Bill/ Antony agreed, in that it showed the shadows rather than showing the leopard. The flour sifting through the door was a sensory detail that would work for anyone who ever picked up a bag of flour. It would suggest the leopard had struck, without showing the injury.

"So, what made a scary monster?" asked the moderator of our panel discussion. Monsters made out of people, was the answer. Bill/ Antony had a particular horror of armies of perfect soldiers, all alike, all specially trained and bred to be superior killing machines. It was natural for someone born between the wars, who had grown to the age of reason during the Second World War, to have this fear. He found the idea of cloned armies genetically bred for slaughter to be particularly horrifying. We talked about books like Frank Herbert's Hellstrom's Hive, with specialized breeders producing armies of cloned soldiers.

When he paused, I spoke up then. "I want to reassure you that no one would ever spend the hundreds of thousands of dollars per soldier to clone an army of perfect soldiers," I said. "It's so much cheaper just to gather up a bunch of kids and train them and discard the culls. You can spend what money you have on weapons. That's what happens in Africa, in Cambodia, and in Central Asian countries. The kind of leader who spends freely the lives of armies doesn't mind discarding the culls along the way. Think of Orson Scott Card's novel Ender's Game, but with a higher death rate among the children. Conceiving the genetic supersoldiers is more affordably done by choosing a few studs to impregnate women than by gestating cloned embryos in artificial wombs. Hitler is credited with doing this – selecting some Aryan soldiers to breed with many women. No one is sure exactly how many children were the result, but the Third Reich didn't last long enough for them to grow up to become the next generation of soldiers."

One of the audience asked if these people born of selective breeding were still alive, and if so, where they were. "Anyone born as a result of this eugenics program isn't talking about it now," I said. "They're just trying to live a normal life among the rest of the Germans born in their generation. Many of them don't know who their fathers were."

The next panelist approached by our moderator was Robyn Herrington. Her day job was as a graphics designer at the University of Calgary Press. She was a short story writer who had picked up the hobby of glassblowing. For Robyn, the most frightening monsters were those among us, roaming typical suburban settings. That's where we live, or at least we can relate to people living there. She spoke of the stereotypical interview that neighbours give to the news media after the serial killer is arrested, saying "But he was a quiet man!" As far as Robyn was concerned, in a story with a fantasy setting such as a pseudo-medieval place or another planet, the monsters are competing with the background for our attention. This competition distracts the reader from the monster. That was why in recently-written books, there were so many vampire and werewolf stories being set in real or realistic modern cities and towns. These stories let readers put the proper focus on the monster.

An audience member mentioned that frightening monsters are those which act with intelligence. Godzilla just stomped around, blindly roaring and thrashing. Far more frightening were the cold and calculating humanoid monsters like zombies that were out to get you. Robyn agreed. She also observed that there were wanna-be vampires and werewolves wandering around at this very convention. People were paying dentists to give them pointed teeth. A few plastic surgeons were creating real pointed ears. No costume necessary. She didn't like the thought that soon people could buy medical treatments to become even more like werewolves and vampires.

"I want to reassure you that there is no need to fear that someone will make real vampires and real werewolves," I said. "There is no need to invent man-made vampires or hormone-created werewolves when there are a few people already who function very effectively AS vampires do and AS werewolves do. These serial killers and bush-living wildmen do not need to have mystic qualities or pointy ears or surgery and medical treatments to do the monster thing. Also, there are people in Caribbean nations treating slave workers as zombies," I added, "with and without the aid of voodoo drugs such as zombie cucumber... mystic qualities not necessary." My fellow panellists agreed, citing the names and stories of infamous serial killers, as well as theories that perhaps many sasquatches and Jersey devils were just wild-living humans gone feral.

"It's also worth pointing out that it's not necessary for me to be bitten by Dracula in order for me to get infected with the idea that it's all right to sustain myself with the life and resources that ought to be sustaining dozens of other people. There's a reason vampire fiction is so popular in the Western nations," I said. "We are eroticising the vampiric nature of our national economies, like romance novelists eroticising their characters falling in love with difficult men."

Our moderator then asked the panellists about what we imagined the future would be like for monsters themselves. What would the monsters look like and be like? Fantasy novelist Rebecca Bradley took the point on this question. Like Robyn, Rebecca was another Calgary-based author.

Rebecca said that she figured that the monsters of the future would be tiny manufactured things like viruses or nanotechnology. It would be hard to defend against these miniature monsters or even to detect them. They would be made things, created on purpose to cause sickness and death. They wouldn't be naturally evolved like the diseases such as influenza or tuberculosis that we humans have caught from contact with our domesticated animals. Rebecca mentioned the rumours circulating when AIDS was being discovered, still-persistent rumours that the disease had been created in a lab to target homosexuals. Some of us in the crowd wore small loops of red ribbon pinned to our clothes as a visible reminder of those who were dying from AIDS. The thought of manufactured disease viruses was particularly awful for Rebecca, especially one such as an airborne Ebola-type virus with a long latency period.

Someone coughed in the back of the room as Rebecca fell silent. There was a wave of nervous laughter through the audience – coughing! Germs! Aah! Then Rebecca looked expectantly at me as the rest grew quiet. I said gently, "I want to reassure you that there is no need to fear that someone will invent new diseases for germ warfare in a lab." The room erupted in laughter again.

"There is no need to fear the creation of new diseases for germ warfare, not when the spores of anthrax are waiting in the ground in the foothills of the Rocky Mountains only a few miles away, within sight of where we are gathered here in Calgary." There were some questions then about the nature of anthrax and its use as a weapon. "Canada and North America have a history of using germ warfare," I pointed out. "Smallpox was deliberately given to the Indians, back East through gifts of infected blankets and in BC through the authorities' withholding of the moderately-effective preventatives just becoming available." Each of the adults in the room had a scar on our arms, a lingering sign of smallpox vaccination, but our children were not being vaccinated. "Smallpox is being prepared again as a tool of disease warfare," I added. "A few vials of smallpox have been preserved for this very function in some scattered labs. There are UN labs which preserve portions adding up to the entire smallpox genome after the last few official samples of smallpox were destroyed."

One of our panellists then asked our moderator what was the thing that scared him? Apart from asking each of us in turn a few questions, he'd been quiet. He still spoke quietly as he answered. He was afraid that evil people would attempt to destroy the world's ecosystem. There was a novel by John Wyndham, No Blade of Grass, in which all the grasses and grains were killed by a disease that had been created to get rid of weeds. The moderator felt that people who wanted to make changes like this were doing evil, whether they were comic-book villains who wanted to destroy the world, or people who just didn't care about the effects of their actions. They would bring on an ice age, and freeze all the water solid. Or they would cause extinctions of all the plants and animals, and the few people left alive would be eating nothing but algae. Or maybe they would set off a cobalt bomb, like the one in the film Beyond the Planet of the Apes, that would set off a chain reaction blowing the entire crust off the Earth.

Then he looked at me expectantly. "I want to reassure you that it is entirely unnecessary to imagine that it would take anyone's malicious and destructive plans to destroy the world's ecosystem," I said, and we all laughed again. It was good to release tension after thinking of his global fear.

"We don't have to make that up, not when the ordinary actions of human civilisation are very effectively changing the world's ecosystem around us right now and have very probably delayed the return of the next Ice Age," I said. "The Ice Ages are cyclical, and we're living in an interglacial interval. The next Ice Age is overdue already, overdue by approximately the same amount of time as humans have used agriculture. The tools of agriculture, grazing animals and tilling earth, are sufficient to change the ecosystem, independent of any malicious intent. The tyrannical vision of malice is unnecessary because the tyranny of civilisation is enough to have the effect we fear. Remember, humans deforested the hills of New Brunswick and Nova Scotia with axes and handsaws – no modern logging techniques necessary!

Pollution from modern civilisation is speeding up the change, but it's been happening for thousands of years, making deserts in Africa, the Middle East, and Tibet."

At this point, there came a question from the audience. All these things the other writers were afraid of – that we all were afraid of – I had just told them that these things were happening, more or less. What was the thing that scared me? "Harm to my children," I said, and swallowed. "And it happened when my son was injured and my daughter saw it happen." There was a murmur of sympathy, and Robyn patted my hand. "I wrote about this injury at the request of the editor of my memoir, my nonfiction book of essays on parenting. That chapter we called 'Welcome to Parent Hell.' It became the core of the book and the single thing I have written which has received the most reader response."

The effect of this discussion was profound on all the panellists; the audience participated enthusiastically and I still have people come up to me at ConVersion and other conventions who remember The Future Of Monsters discussion. Each time a panellist spoke, and I answered them, the audience's engagement with the topic and enjoyment of our dialogue increased. The point throughout was not "Be Afraid of Bad Things That Are Happening" but "What Scares Us? How Do We Think and Talk About It? What can we as writers do with the things that scare us?"

And in discussing why we are scared of unrealistic fantasy ideas, we came to understand that at least part of the reason is because these ideas are not unreal – they can and do happen in real life. Part of why we talk and write about these ideas is to acknowledge that these things can and do happen. Another reason we write about these ideas is to put the events safely in the past: it happened, but it happened in the past and it's over now and we survived. We also discussed the distancing of these real fears into fiction: it happened to somebody else, a made-up character, not me, not my family. I will demonize the thing or person

I fear because it couldn't be part of the real humanity I associate with myself. The fear will be safely external.

We spoke of the best moment in George Lucas' entire body of film work. It was a scene in The Empire Strikes Back, where Luke decapitates Vader and sees his own face inside the mask. And before the panel discussion broke up, we spoke also of the writer Anthony Burgess who wrote in Clockwork Orange a scene of a brutal home invasion. He wrote the scene based on an invasion of his own home in which his wife was raped. The genius element in that scene was writing about the experience from the viewpoint of one of the attackers. It was a brilliant decision, one I think few of us writers could make.

Of course, Burgess had been told by his doctor that he had about a year to live because of brain cancer. It is a marvellously focusing thing, to be told that one may die soon. It is particularly focusing for an intellectual to be diagnosed with a fatal brain cancer. Burgess was desperate to leave some kind of money behind to support his widow. He had to write books now, right now, and he did – at least four of them within a year. He never expected to outlive the diagnosis by more than thirty years.

It's not only the famous professional writers whose lives surprise them. Just under a year after that panel discussion at ConVersion, we lost Bill. William Antony Swithin Sarjeant was dead of cancer at sixty-seven. That's not nearly old enough for such a grand man.

Some of us live longer than we ever expected to live. Days after that panel discussion at ConVersion, Robyn Harrington went to Worldcon. There, her novel caught the interest of an editor wearing a loud tie, an editor at one of the big genre publishers. She was on her way home by plane when she sneezed wrong somehow, and wrenched her back. X-rays to figure out that injury led to the discovery that she had cancer. Robyn had nearly three more years of grace, and rushed to get so much done in her life and for other writers because of that lucky painful sneeze. She lived longer than expected. And it still wasn't nearly enough, damnitt. The short story workshop and contest at ConVersion are named as a memorial to her.

Some of us live years we never expected to see. When we met for that panel discussion, Rebecca Bradley had just been given a writer's grant from the Alberta Foundation for the Arts. She was able to spend the next five months writing the core stories for her oddball collection The Lateral Truth, but it took five years to find a publisher. If you want to think about what scares you, think about that part. Think about five years trying to find a publisher. And that's even though she had already sold two other story collections and a fantasy trilogy. If that doesn't scare you, you're not paying attention. And if you can't write that fear into a horror story, you're not trying.

And years go by, and the flare of silver hair that bloomed at my temple with my hearing loss has spread as my hearing continues to fade. I continued to write stories and novels that caught the attention of the editor with the loud ties. Only later did I learn at least part of the reason his replies were so delayed and part of why he was unable to imagine how to market any of my novels. He had an assistant who blithely hid at home many of the manuscripts so they wouldn't have to be dealt with at work. I can't make that up. I write for a living, and I've been an editor's assistant, and I just can't make that up.

But by then, I had been introduced to another editor for an educational press. Over six years, I wrote for them two dozen short books on science, health, and literature, and a novel for an emerging press. I work as a labourer to supplement the modest income from writing. If you want to think about what scares you, think about that part, too. Think about coming up on fifty years old, writing three or four books a year and still having to haul boxes and clean toilets in order to live like a student. And that's not the scary part.

The scary part is learning how to write about my hearing loss and migraines so that a doctor, neurologist, and ear doctor actually read the notes. The scary part is looking into an MRI machine as my brain is scanned for the third time in thirty years. These scans have hammered me with noise, magnetic fields and radiation. They show nothing out of place, no tumor or blood vessel to blame for my time-share in pain and stupidity, only reactions among vanishingly small amounts of chemicals in my nerves like angels dancing on the point of a pin. The scary part is the realization that I am the lucky one among us four writers on that panel discussion of how to write about what scares us.

Also by Paula Johanson

Prime Ministers of Canada
Pierre Elliott Trudeau: Child of Nature
Charles Tupper: Warhorse

Standalone
Small Rain and Other Nightmares
Island Views
Plum Tree
Tower in the Crooked Wood
King Kwong: Larry Kwong, the China Clipper Who Broke the NHL
Colour Barrier
Science Critters

Watch for more at paulajohanson.blogspot.com.

About the Author

Paula Johanson is a Canadian writer. A graduate of the University of Victoria with an MA in Canadian literature, she has worked as a security guard, a short order cook, a teacher, newspaper writer, and more. As well as editing books and teaching materials, she has run an organic-method small farm with her spouse, raised gifted twins, and cleaned university dormitories. In addition to novels and stories, she is the author of forty-two books written for educational publishers, among them *The Paleolithic Revolution* and *Women Writers* from the series *Defying Convention: Women Who Changed The World.* Johanson is an active member of SF Canada, the national association of science fiction and fantasy authors.

Read more at paulajohanson.blogspot.com.